King
To
Spare

An International Thriller

Max Barrington

Copyright © 2024 Max Barrington layout design and Copyright © 2024 by MPH Holding Published in 2024 by Etteleah cover and art by MPH Holding

This book is a work of fiction. Unless otherwise indicated, all the names, characters, businesses, places, events and incidents in this book are either the product of the author's imagination or used in a fictitious manner. Any resemblance to actual persons, living or dead, or actual events and/or places is purely coincidental.

All rights reserved. No part of this book may be reproduced or transmitted in any form or by any means, electronic or mechanical, including photocopying, recording, or by information storage and retrieval system, without the author's permission

For the love of my life,
my darling wife and my inspiration,
Lynette

First published in Australia in 2024 by Etteleah Books - Cairns Australia
This copy published in 2025

Contents

Max Barrington

He walks through palaces yet dreams of freedom, blind to the truth that many would give everything just to live a day in his shoes.

Avalanche!

Avalanches are not uncommon in the mountains near St. Moritz, Switzerland. The region's steep slopes and frequent snowfall create the perfect conditions for sudden and unpredictable slides. One such avalanche occurred on a January day in a year when the newly throned monarch, along with his wife and their children, had chosen to forgo their usual stay at a chalet near Verbier. Instead, they had opted for the privacy of a secluded chalet near Piz Corvatsch.

It was one of those indicators that went unnoticed, until it was too late. A miscalculation, an oversight, or simply nature's unpredictability had allowed a dangerous buildup of wind-driven snow to remain undisturbed. Normally, controlled detonations using gas-based systems are employed to dislodge unstable snow accumulations before they pose a threat. However, detecting these instabilities requires a trained eye, as even the slightest changes in snow contours can signal impending danger. The process demands close observation, which in itself is a perilous task in such an unforgiving environment.

In this instance, the warning signs were either missed or underestimated, and what followed was an event that would not be forgotten. Steps would be taken to ensure such an oversight would never happen again.

The aftermath was nothing short of devastating. The sheer scale of destruction defied description, leaving behind a scene of chaos and sorrow. The avalanche had shown no mercy, its force indiscriminate, claiming the lives of many, royalty and commoners alike. The loss was staggering, and the impact was felt across the nation.

As news of the tragedy spread, the country was plunged into mourning. A ten-day period of national grief was declared, with flags lowered to half-mast and public events postponed out of respect for the fallen. The royal house of Wynasleigh, bound by tradition and personal loss, observed an additional seven days of mourning in solemn remembrance. Across the land, tributes poured in, candles flickered in the windows of mourning citizens, and the weight of collective sorrow settled over the kingdom like a heavy snowfall, silent yet profound.

King Albert III was dead, along with his heirs. The line of succession had been shattered in an instant, leaving the monarchy in a precarious and unprecedented state of uncertainty. With no direct heirs remaining, attention turned to the next viable candidates.

The most immediate option was Albert's next youngest brother, Prince James. However, James had long since distanced himself from royal life, renouncing his duties and responsibilities in favour of a quiet existence in America. He had no interest in the monarchy, having deliberately removed himself from its constraints years ago. His disinterest was well known, and given his firm stance, he was not a feasible candidate to ascend the throne.

That left the course of natural succession to fall to Prince Arnold, who, at the tender age of just twenty-three, now found himself the rightful heir. Unlike his elder brother James, who had distanced himself from royal duties, Arnold had spent his life firmly within the royal fold, eagerly embracing tradition and responsibility. From a young age, he had harboured ambitions of leadership, meticulously preparing for the day he would ascend the throne.

But there was one formidable obstacle standing in his path, his father, King Alexander IV.

In an audacious and unprecedented move, the former king had, of his own volition, reclaimed the throne, disregarding the established order of succession. His actions were entirely unsanctioned, yet no one had dared to challenge him. Who, after all, would stand in the way of a king who refused to abdicate his power?

Not a single figure within the court held the authority to depose him. And collectively, there was no one brave enough to make the attempt.

The only entity with the legal power to challenge the former king was Parliament, the sole governing body capable of enforcing his removal. However, in a cruel twist of irony, for Parliament to act, they would first need the king's own advice and consent.

And King Alexander IV had made his stance abundantly clear, he had no intention of stepping aside and claimed it to be a 'caretaking' role.

Alexander IV had only recently abdicated the throne in favour of Albert, believing that his elder son was best suited to lead the nation. The idea of Arnold now taking the crown was something he could not accept. Whether due to personal misgivings, political concerns, or a deep-seated belief that Arnold was, in Alexander IV's eyes, wholly unfit to rule. Whether due to his temperament, lack of political acumen, or some deeper personal failing, the former king was resolute in his opposition. He would do everything in his power to prevent his younger son from ascending the throne, even if it meant defying tradition and reshaping the monarchy's future.

Yet there was one immutable truth: abdication was final. Once a monarch had relinquished the throne, there was no simple path back. The only way for Alexander IV to reclaim his position legitimately and legally, was through an act of Parliament, an extraordinary and unprecedented step that would shake the very foundations of the kingdom. Would he dare pursue such a course? And if not, who would ultimately wear the crown?

Alex, Alexander IV, convened an urgent meeting with his most trusted advisors to discuss the possibility of reclaiming the crown. Though his abdication had been final, there remained one narrow path forward: a formal act of Parliament. It was an unprecedented move, but desperate times called for desperate measures.

The counsel he received was surprisingly favourable, at least in terms of strategy. While the likelihood of success remained uncertain, one undeniable advantage emerged, the sheer length of the parliamentary process. A decision of such magnitude could take a year or more to debate, draft, and ratify. In the intricate web of politics and procedure, delays were inevitable, and that was exactly what Alexander needed. Time.

Time to manoeuvre, to influence key figures, to sow doubt about Arnold's suitability for the throne. Time to rally support among those within the government and the aristocracy who shared his misgivings. Time to ensure that, when the moment of reckoning arrived, the monarchy would not fall into the hands of a ruler he deemed unworthy.

For Alexander IV, the path was clear. He did not need an immediate victory, he simply needed to keep the crown out of Arnold's grasp long enough for an alternative to emerge. And with Parliament caught in the slow grind of bureaucracy, time was, for now, on his side.

Alex's thoughts now turned to Arnold. It was deeply saddening, such a shame, that his youngest son had become so completely estranged from both him and his wife, Charmaine. What should have been a close and enduring bond between parent and child had been severed, replaced by distance, resentment, and silence.

To Alex and Charmaine, there was no mystery as to the cause of this painful rift. They placed the blame squarely on Arnold's partner, the person they believed had driven a wedge between father and son. What had begun as subtle shifts in Arnold's behaviour had escalated into full-blown alienation, spreading like a contagion through the entire royal family.

Where once there had been warmth, there was now cold detachment. Family gatherings had become tense and infrequent, private conversations strained or nonexistent. Arnold had changed, not just in attitude, but in loyalty. It was as if he had been slowly pulled away, drawn into the influence of someone who, in Alex's view, had no respect for the monarchy, its traditions, or the duty that came with their lineage.And now, that same estranged son was poised to take the throne. The mere thought filled Alex with dread. A monarch should be steadfast, unwavering in duty, and wholly committed to the crown. But Arnold was no longer the boy Alex had raised, he had become a man shaped by forces beyond his father's control. Shaped by the influence of an insidious and bitter man, Melvin Clarkson.

From the moment he had entered Arnold's life, Alex and Charmaine had recognised him for what he was, a disruptor, a man with ambition that far exceeded his place. Melvin had eventually married Arnold, but not with his father's grace or blessing, but secretly as such approval would never have been given. He was a commoner, his lineage lacking the nobility required to integrate into the royal family. The monarchy had rules, traditions that spanned generations, and Melvin was an outsider in every sense.

But Melvin had not needed royal approval, he had needed only Arnold. Slowly, methodically, he had drawn him away, poisoning his mind against his own family. He had nurtured his growing resentment, convincing him that his parents' opposition was not out of duty to the crown but out of personal malice, out of an outdated and elitist refusal to accept change. And Arnold, blinded by love, or perhaps by manipulation, had believed him.

Alex had watched helplessly as his son became distant, then defiant, and finally a stranger. His pleas had fallen on deaf ears, his warnings dismissed as arrogance. And now, the damage was done. Arnold was no longer a devoted son or a prince bound to duty. He was a man prepared to claim a throne that, in Alex's eyes, he neither respected nor deserved, all under the influence of a man who had no place in the monarchy's legacy.

Deep down, Alex realised that he was only biding time and that his son would become King, but he had yet one more plan, a contingency plan that was known by only himself.

The email left no room for ambiguity, Mathew was to collect a one-way ticket from the British Airlines desk at Melbourne International Airport at precisely 2:00 pm on the following Saturday afternoon. There were no explanations, no pleasantries, just a simple directive.

Today was Monday. That gave him less than a week to get his affairs in order, but for Mathew, that wasn't a problem.

His girlfriend had recently returned to Australia for a break from her work in Cape Town, which meant she would be around if anything urgent needed attention. His mother's apartment was conveniently located in the same high-rise building as his own, offering an additional layer of reassurance. Not that there was much to worry about, his home required no special care in his absence, and there were no pets, plants, or lingering obligations to tie him down.

His work situation posed no issue either. As a legal consultant who took on cases on a contract basis, he wasn't bound to any long-term commitments. There were no deadlines looming over him, no clients waiting on his advice. He could simply walk away, at least for now.

In many ways, the timing couldn't have been better. And yet, despite the ease with which he could leave, the weight of the unknown settled heavily on his shoulders. The summons had come, as he had always been told it might. Now, all that remained was for him to decide whether he was truly ready to answer it.

As he reread the email, a sense of urgency settled over him. The details of the trip, its purpose, its destination, remained a mystery, but one thing was clear: there was no room for hesitation. Whatever lay ahead, Mathew had been given his instructions by a person known to him only as AW, and now, all he could do was prepare.

From the day he had turned twenty-one, he had been warned that a call might come, one that would change everything. But in the ten years that had passed since, he had never truly believed it would happen. It had felt more like a distant possibility, a shadowy threat lurking at the edges of his otherwise ordinary life.

That warning had come alongside a revelation that had shaken the very foundation of his existence. He was not just Mathew, the man he had always believed himself to be. He was the illegitimate son of King Alexander IV.

His mother had never spoken of his father, and for most of his life, he hadn't questioned their extraordinary comfort. They had never wanted for anything. A generous stipend had sustained them for as long as he could remember, beginning even before his birth. It had provided them with a standard of living far beyond what they could have otherwise afforded.

He had been told that the wealth came from a benefactor known only to him as "AW." The arrangement had been simple: the money would continue to flow, ensuring a life of ease, but one day, there might be a price to pay. One day, he might be called upon to earn what he had been given.

Now, as he stared at the email instructing him to collect a one-way ticket, he knew that day had finally arrived.

Mathew, now a striking man in his early thirties, possessed a rugged handsomeness that set him apart. His strong, chiseled features carried the weathered look of someone who had seen and done more than his years might suggest. His short cropped hair only added to his commanding presence.

Standing at an imposing 1,880 millimetres, or six feet two inches in the old scale, he carried himself with the confidence of a man who knew his own strength. Though not obsessed with fitness, he maintained a solid, athletic build, the result of a disciplined routine rather than vanity. There was an energy about him, a quiet intensity that hinted at a sharp mind and a relentless drive.

During his childhood in a quiet Canberra suburb, Mathew had always felt a little different, though he couldn't quite put his finger on why. There was an ever-present sense of being on the outside looking in, a feeling that became more pronounced as he grew older.

It was during his primary school years that the questions began to surface, not just in his own mind, but from his classmates as well. Why did he never mention his father? Why was there no dad at school events, no father-son outings, no stories shared about weekend adventures or family holidays?

Whenever the subject arose, his mother's response was always the same, delivered with quiet firmness and a gentle but unyielding finality.

"It was quite a while ago when we lost him," she would say. "And although he will always be in our hearts, we no longer speak of him."

There was never any elaboration, no details, no space for further questioning. It was a script she had perfected, a barrier she had built to keep the past where she wanted it, buried.

And so, Mathew learned to stop asking. But the silence surrounding his father only deepened the mystery, and as the years passed, that unanswered question would shape him in ways he could never have imagined.

Each day at school, Mathew never had to worry about lunch. He always carried ample money to buy whatever he wanted from the canteen, a small luxury he took for granted. It wasn't until he grew older that he started noticing subtle differences between himself and his classmates.

His uniform always seemed cleaner and brighter than theirs, though he hadn't given it much thought at the time. What he didn't realise was that his mother replaced his school clothes every three months, ensuring they never showed signs of wear. His school shoes were refreshed just as frequently, always polished and unscuffed, while his friends often wore the same pair for the entire year, sometimes longer.

He had almost everything he wanted, rarely having to ask twice. His mother was generous, ensuring he lacked for nothing. Yet, despite their comfortable lifestyle, she was determined that he would not grow up taking money for granted. As soon as he was old enough, she arranged for him to take a casual job at the local mini-market.

"To give you an appreciation of the value of money," she had told him.

Though at first, he saw it as just another of his mother's rules, Mathew soon found that he genuinely enjoyed the part-time work. It gave him a sense of independence, a glimpse into the lives of others, and, most importantly, a growing awareness of just how privileged he truly was.

Throughout his primary school years and well into the first two years of high school, there was one thing Mathew absolutely despised, his twice-weekly piano lessons. His mother had insisted on them, enforcing the routine with unwavering determination, no matter how much he protested.

It wasn't that he lacked musical ability; in fact, his teacher often praised his natural talent. But to Mathew, the lessons felt like a tedious chore, an unwelcome interruption to his afternoons when he would have much rather been outside with his friends. While other kids were kicking a footy around or racing their bikes through the neighbourhood, he was stuck indoors, drilling scales and perfecting pieces he had no interest in playing.

No amount of pleading or complaints could sway his mother. "One day, you'll thank me," she would say, brushing aside his frustration with the quiet certainty of someone who believed she knew best.

At the time, he couldn't imagine ever feeling grateful for those endless hours at the piano bench. But life had a way of making sense of things in hindsight, something Mathew would come to realise in the not-too-distant future.

By his later years of high school, when weekend parties stretched into two-day events, his once-despised piano skills became an unexpected asset. Invitations were never in short supply, everyone wanted Mathew there, especially when word got around about his talent for jazz improvisations. While others fumbled through the usual teenage small talk, he could effortlessly command a room with the piano, weaving lively rhythms and smooth melodies that had people gathered around, listening, singing, and clapping along.

Had he wanted to, Mathew could have built an endless social circle, collecting acquaintances wherever he went. But his mother, ever watchful and quietly deliberate in shaping his life, ensured that didn't happen. Through careful and discreet influence, she guided him toward a select group, keeping his friendships limited to just two close companions, ones she deemed trustworthy and suitable. One of the companions, a young man who was suffering from Asperger's syndrome, absolutely idolised Mathew. Mathew's mother had identified the symptoms thanks to her advanced clinical studies of that and similar symptoms and disease's.

At the time, he hadn't questioned it. But later, as he came to understand more about his past, he would wonder just how much of his life had truly been his own, and how much had been orchestrated from the shadows.

After completing high school, Mathew was enrolled in the Australian Defence Force Academy, where he undertook a rigorous academic and military training program. He studied law through the University of New South Wales, balancing the demands of legal education with the discipline and structure of military life.

Upon graduation, he advanced to the Royal Military College, Duntroon, where he completed his officer training and was commissioned as a Lieutenant. From there, he joined the Australian Army Legal Corps, a highly specialised branch responsible for providing legal support to the military.

With his formal legal education complete, Mathew was admitted to practice as a legal practitioner, a milestone that not only solidified

     Max Barrington

his career but also positioned him within an elite group of legal professionals who operated within the complexities of military law. His role would require him to navigate everything from military justice and operational law to advising commanders on the legal implications of their decisions, responsibilities that would test both his intellect and his resolve in ways he had never imagined.

It was during his military training that Mathew reached the age at which it had been decided he would finally be given full disclosure of his royal heritage. However, unlike what one might expect, the revelation did not come as a complete shock.

For years, Mathew had been piecing things together, collecting small but significant clues that had, at first, seemed like nothing more than passing remarks from his mother. She had always been careful, never explicitly revealing too much, but occasionally dropping hints, veiled in casual conversation, as if by accident. A comment here, an unusual reference there, each one had lingered in his mind, slowly forming a puzzle he hadn't quite been able to complete.

By the time the truth was formally presented to him, it was more of a confirmation than a revelation. Deep down, he had already suspected there was something extraordinary about his past, something that set him apart from those around him. Now, with the truth finally laid bare, the weight of his lineage settled upon him, bringing with it both privilege and responsibility, two things he had never sought, yet could no longer ignore.

Mathew was encouraged to pursue his career, whether within the military or in private legal practice. Regardless of which path he chose, his stipend would continue, ensuring that financial security was never a concern. In addition to this ongoing support, he would also receive remuneration through his profession, allowing him to establish himself independently while still benefiting from the arrangements that had been in place since before his birth.

However, there was one unyielding condition, an ironclad rule that could not be negotiated. Under no circumstances was Mathew permitted to marry. Should he choose to do so, the consequences would be absolute and irreversible. His stipend would be revoked immediately, along with any other privileges, financial support, or obligations that had been extended to him. It was not simply a matter of wealth; it was a matter of lineage, discretion, and the carefully maintained secrecy surrounding his true heritage.

Despite this restriction, he was not expected to live a solitary life. He was free to have a girlfriend, enjoy companionship, or even engage in a long-term de facto relationship. The line was drawn only at marriage, a boundary that had been set long before he was even aware of its existence. The reasoning behind it remained largely unspoken, but Mathew understood that his place in the world was not entirely his own to define. There were forces at play, decisions made in corridors of power he had never walked, that dictated the terms of his life in ways few could truly comprehend. He found himself unexpectedly drawn to these secretive revelations, almost relishing the intrigue that surrounded them. What had once felt like a burden, an unknown shadow looming over his life, was now becoming something he actively sought to unravel. Each new piece of information added another layer to the complex puzzle of his existence, and with every revelation, he felt a strange sense of exhilaration.

It was as if he had been living in a carefully crafted illusion, only now beginning to see the intricate design beneath it. The secrecy, the unspoken rules, the carefully orchestrated hints from his mother, all of it had been leading to this moment. And rather than feeling overwhelmed, he found himself intrigued, eager to uncover the full extent of the truth that had been kept from him for so long.

When Mathew arrived at the airport to collect his airline ticket, he was surprised to find a small brown padded bag handed to him along with the ticket. On the front of the package was a simple note, written in bold letters: "Open immediately."

Curious, he carefully peeled off the tape and opened the bag. Inside, nestled in soft protective padding, was an iPhone 16. It was sleek and shiny, the latest model, unmistakably high-end. On the front screen of the phone was another note, this one on a small Post-it: "Turn on."

Mathew hesitated for only a moment before following the instruction. His fingers brushed the screen, and the phone came to life, its bright display illuminating the darkened corner of the terminal. He was left with an unsettling feeling, this wasn't just a gift or a random piece of technology. It was a deliberate action. Finding a seat in a reasonably quiet area Mathew powered up the telephone which immediately rang, before he had a chance to say 'Hello" a voice commanded him to go immediately to the Qantas Club reception where the voice would meet him.

After having to ask directions to the club's reception area, Mathew soon arrived at his destination. The receptionist, flashing a warm smile, asked for his name and checked him off on her guest list before gesturing towards the entry doors.

As he approached, a man of similar build and height to Mathew appeared alongside him, offering a polite nod. "Good afternoon, sir. Shall we go inside, and I shall formally introduce myself?" the man said with a slight but assured tone.

Intrigued but still somewhat uncertain, Mathew followed the stranger to a vacant section of the lounge, where two plush lounge chairs were arranged around a circular drinks table. The atmosphere was sophisticated yet unassuming. The stranger raised his hand, catching the attention of a nearby steward. "What will you have to drink, sir?" he asked as he gestured for Mathew to take a seat.

Once their drinks were ordered, the man finally introduced himself. "I'm Callum Gibb, sir. I am your equerry," he said with a slight nod of his head, though he didn't offer a handshake.

Mathew, slightly taken aback by the formal title, extended his hand anyway. "Mathew Jeffries-Wynn," he replied, shaking Callum's hand firmly. "Your... what? I'm sorry, could you repeat that?"

Callum's eyes softened in a manner that suggested he was used to this reaction. "Equerry, sir... sort of a personal assistant," he clarified, his voice steady but polite. "I'm afraid you'll have to put up with me for the time being."

Mathew raised an eyebrow, still processing the unexpected turn his life had taken. Callum continued, explaining the breadth of his role in greater detail, but also revealing a few more intriguing tidbits.

"I'm a Lieutenant Commander in the Royal Navy," Callum added, his tone cool and matter-of-fact. "But we are not alone here. The gentleman to your right, for example, is an MI5 officer."

Mathew turned his head slightly, his curiosity piqued. "And who's the gentleman returning from the bar with two Cokes?"

Callum smiled faintly. "Also MI5," he said, giving a subtle nod towards the man as he approached, "it's no good introducing them as they change over all the time, I am notified each time there is a change" Callum indicated to the ear piece he was wearing.

The revelation left Mathew both awestruck and slightly apprehensive. His life, it seemed, was unfolding in ways he could never have anticipated. As they boarded the plane and made their way to their first-class seats, Callum stepped back slightly, allowing Mathew to slide into the window seat before settling in beside him. The cabin exuded an air of quiet luxury, with plush seats and an attentive crew ensuring a seamless experience.

Once they were comfortably seated, Callum turned to Mathew with a relaxed smile. "I am officially off duty until we arrive in Abu Dhabi in fifteen hours' time. Allow me to shout you a drink, sir!"

Mathew smirked and shook his head. "Enough of this 'sir' shit," he said with a chuckle. "It's Mathew or Mat. And yes, I think a bourbon and Coke would go down well. Thanks, Callum."

Callum gave a slight nod, signalling to the flight attendant as he leaned back in his seat. "Bourbon and Coke it is, Mat."

With the hum of the engines in the background and the anticipation of what lay ahead, Mathew allowed himself a moment to take it all in.

By the time they landed in Abu Dhabi, Mathew had been made aware of the demise of King Albert III. He recalled hearing about the tragedy at the time, though, in hindsight, the news reports had seemed unusually low-key for an event of such magnitude, an avalanche that had wiped out the reigning monarch and his entire family. It was the kind of catastrophe that should have dominated global headlines for weeks, yet it had been handled with an almost calculated restraint.

As they disembarked and made their way through the terminal, Mathew turned to Callum, his curiosity now bordering on frustration. "Why am I being taken to England?" he asked, his tone edged with suspicion. "What's going on?"

Callum let out a short sigh, adjusting the strap of his carry-on before answering. "Don't know," he said, though the slight hesitation in his voice didn't go unnoticed. "And even if I did, I most likely wouldn't be able to tell you." He offered Mathew an apologetic look. "Sorry about all this secrecy, but it's got nothing to do with me… honestly."

Mathew studied him for a moment, searching for any sign of deception, but Callum's expression remained neutral, professional. It was clear he had been trained to say as little as possible.

"Right," Mathew muttered, rubbing a hand over his face. "So I just keep blindly following orders, is that it?"

Callum gave a small shrug. "For now, yes. But trust me, you'll get your answers soon enough."

Mathew wasn't so sure. Something about the way all of this was unfolding felt deliberately vague, as though he were being manoeuvred into position for something far bigger than he had been led to believe. And that, more than anything, unsettled him.

Upon their arrival in London, Mathew and Callum were swiftly ushered into a waiting black sedan, its windows tinted to obscure the occupants from prying eyes. The drive through the city was smooth and efficient, bypassing the usual congestion as though prearranged. Within minutes, they arrived at The Lanesborough, an opulent five-star hotel overlooking Hyde Park, where the car pulled up to the entrance with practiced precision.

As they stepped inside, they were immediately greeted by the hotel's Majordomo, a distinguished man in a perfectly tailored suit who exuded an air of quiet authority. Without hesitation, he guided them towards a private elevator, swiping a keycard to access the restricted upper floors.

The doors slid open on level six, revealing an MI5 agent standing sentinel just outside the lift. His posture was rigid, his expression unreadable, but his sharp eyes took in every detail of Mathew and Callum with the efficiency of a man trained to assess threats in an instant. As they stepped into the corridor, two additional agents emerged from a nearby suite, having just completed a final security sweep. They exchanged brief nods with Callum, who, listening intently to the feed in his earpiece, received the all-clear to proceed.

Mathew's suite was nothing short of exquisite, spacious yet meticulously arranged, exuding an understated elegance that balanced comfort with grandeur. The living area featured a plush lounge set before an antique fireplace, with a small dining table that would seat four, positioned beneath a crystal chandelier. A kitchenette, stocked with fine china and polished silverware, and a fully stocked bar occupied one corner, while an adjoining bedroom boasted a king-sized bed, draped in high-thread-count linens. The en suite bathroom gleamed with marble and gold fixtures, fit for royalty, which, Mathew realised with unease, might be precisely the point.

A discreet, connecting door led to the adjoining room, Callum's quarters. A necessary arrangement, no doubt, ensuring that his newly appointed equerry was always within reach.

Mathew took a slow breath, absorbing the sheer magnitude of his surroundings. Whatever lay ahead, one thing was clear, he was no longer merely an observer in this unfolding saga. He was at the centre of it.

To Mathew's horror, Callum began unpacking his suitcase with the efficiency of someone well-accustomed to such duties.

"I'll take care of that!" Mathew said, his tone friendly but laced with mild embarrassment.

Callum paused, hands mid-fold, and glanced up with an amused smile. "It's all part of my job, sir," he replied, his voice light yet professional. "But if you'd prefer, "

"Of course, I'd prefer!" Mathew cut in, shaking his head. "I'm sorry, old chap, but I'm not used to being… looked after like this."

"As you wish, sir..." Callum started before catching himself. "I mean, Mat."

They both chuckled at the small but significant adjustment before deciding to check out the hotel bar.

As they walked, Callum briefed Mathew on the following day's schedule. "We have a fitting at Benson & Clegg in the morning. You'll need various formal and ceremonial outfits. I have a list of what's required."

Mathew groaned. "Sounds thrilling."

Callum smirked. "It gets better. You have a pre-luncheon appointment with King Alexander IV at eleven-thirty."

Mathew stopped in his tracks. "With the King?"

"Well, he's no longer really the King since he abdicated, but we all still refer to him as King" Callum confirmed, his tone casual. "After

                                          Max Barrington

that, I have no idea what's planned for you. I just stick around and wait for instructions."

Mathew exhaled sharply, rubbing the back of his neck. "Right. Well, let's get that drink, then. I have a feeling I'm going to need it."

Leaving the tailors on Jermyn Street the next morning, Mathew stepped onto the pavement wearing a perfectly tailored morning suit, his first, but certainly not his last. The crisp lines and fine fabric should have made him feel regal, or at the very least, distinguished. Instead, all he felt was the dull throb of a slight hangover and the weight of what lay ahead.

Meeting His Father

He was on his way to meet his father for the first time.

His father.

The words still felt foreign, surreal. How did one prepare to meet a man they had never known? And not just any man, King Alexander IV of England.

Mathew had spent years piecing together fragments of his past, small clues his mother had left like breadcrumbs. Yet, even after all the whispered hints and cryptic acknowledgments, he had never truly allowed himself to believe it. Now, there was no room for doubt. The truth stood before him, looming as grand and immovable as Buckingham Palace itself.

But it wasn't Buckingham Palace where he was taken.

Instead, the car pulled up in front of an unassuming old building, one that looked more like a post office or a government records office than a place where a king might reside. The architecture was plain, almost deliberately nondescript, its weathered stone façade giving little away. If Mathew hadn't known better, he would have assumed they had arrived at the wrong location.

As they stepped out of the car, Callum turned to him with a nod.

"This is where I leave you, sir," he said. "You're on your own now."

Mathew barely had time to register the words before Callum continued.

"I'll meet you back at the hotel reception later this afternoon. Just follow the instructions given, and you'll be fine."

With that, Callum ushered Mathew through the entrance, into a sparsely furnished waiting room with antique chairs and a large, imposing clock ticking on the wall. Then, just as quickly as he had arrived, Callum was gone, vanishing like a ghost, leaving Mathew alone in a place that felt utterly detached from the grandeur of royalty.

Whatever was about to happen, it was clear that this meeting was shrouded in secrecy.

The waiting room was almost eerily bare, no receptionist, no name plaques, nothing to indicate the importance of what was to come. A few well-worn lounge chairs were arranged neatly, as if rarely used. A side table held glass jugs of water and an assortment of drinking glasses, while another table displayed the day's copy of The London Times and BRM, their crisp pages untouched. The air was thick with quiet anticipation.

Mathew glanced around, debating whether to sit when, without warning, a door at the centre of the room swung open. A man in a dark suit, his demeanour composed and unreadable, stepped inside.

"This way, please, sir," he said softly, his voice polite but firm.

Mathew followed him into an adjoining office, equally unremarkable, yet something about it carried a weight of significance. There were no extravagant furnishings, just a large wooden desk positioned squarely in the middle of the room. Behind it sat a man who, despite his unassuming surroundings, exuded an air of authority.

He was elderly, perhaps in his seventies, with noble, distinguished features and a bearing that suggested years of experience in wielding power. His sharp blue eyes studied Mathew with quiet intensity, as if measuring him up before a word had even been spoken.

Mathew swallowed hard. He knew, without needing an introduction, exactly who this man was.

Callum had briefed him on the proper etiquette, address the King as Your Majesty initially, then Sir in further conversation. He had rehearsed the words in his head, determined to get it right. But before he could even open his mouth, the man behind the desk was already rising from his chair, moving toward him with surprising agility for someone of his years.

"Mathew… Mathew," the King said, his voice rich with emotion. "At last. At long last, we finally meet. I have cherished this moment for so many years."

The warmth in his tone, the way he held out his hand as if to bridge the gap of lost time, caught Mathew off guard. He had expected formality, perhaps even distance, but not this.

Mathew hesitated for only a second before grasping the outstretched hand. His grip was firm, steady, but his voice wavered slightly as he spoke the words that had been burning in his mind since the moment he learned the truth.

"Father?" His voice was quieter than he intended, but the weight of the question was undeniable. "Is it true? Are you really my father?"

The King, without relinquishing his grip on Mathew's hand, placed his left arm gently over his shoulder, a gesture both paternal and reassuring. His eyes, deep and knowing, searched Mathew's face as he spoke, his voice steady but tinged with emotion.

"I understand that you don't know me, Mathew, and I cannot expect you to feel anything for a man who has, until now, been nothing more than a name, a title, a mystery." He exhaled slowly, as if the weight of the years between them pressed heavily upon him. "But believe me when I tell you, I have known you. I have followed your life from the moment you took your first breath to this very moment."

The sincerity in his tone, the quiet conviction in his words, made Mathew's chest tighten. He wanted to resist, to hold onto the distance he had always maintained between himself and the idea of a father he had never known. And yet, standing here, face-to-face with the man who had shaped his existence from the shadows, he felt something shift within him, something unexpected, something unsettling.

He swallowed hard, his mind racing. "Then why?" he asked, his voice barely above a whisper. "Why wait until now?"

"It was simply a political impossibility, an option that never existed," the King said, his tone firm yet not unkind. "And I wouldn't expect you to understand, so I won't even attempt to explain."

He paused for a moment, studying Mathew's expression before continuing. "That said, I have a role for you to fulfil. In this instance, I will hold you under no obligation, you will have the freedom to reject my proposal if you so choose. But before you decide, I ask that you take a seat and hear me out. I will outline what I have in mind, and as time progresses, we can refine the finer details. You'll also have the opportunity to raise any questions over luncheon."

With that, the King gestured toward a chair, and Mathew, curiosity piqued, took his seat. Over the next hour, his father methodically laid out his vision, a future where Mathew would become the heir to the throne.

As the King spoke, Mathew found himself drawn in, his initial skepticism giving way to an undeniable sense of purpose. By the time the discussion concluded, he was no longer merely considering the offer, he was embracing it with enthusiasm, eager to step into the role his father had prepared for him.

After lunch, Mathew was introduced to Malcolm Talbot, one of the King's most experienced procedural advisors. With a wealth of knowledge on royal protocol and tradition, Malcolm was tasked with preparing Mathew for the expectations and responsibilities that came with his newfound position. For the next few hours, Mathew listened intently as Malcolm guided him through the intricate web of royal customs, historical precedents, and the subtle yet critical nuances of courtly conduct. The lessons were dense, but Malcolm's expertise and measured explanations made the information easier to digest.

As evening approached, Mathew's schedule remained full. Just before a light but strategic 'working' dinner, he met with Blair Washington, the head of royal security. Blair's briefing was very formal and extensive, covering not only the security measures for Mathew's upcoming visit to London but also broader concerns about his visibility, public exposure, and the potential risks that came with stepping into the royal spotlight. The gravity of the situation became clear, his life was about to change in ways he hadn't fully anticipated.

With the day's meetings concluded, the King bid Mathew farewell. His expression was one of both expectation and reassurance. "We'll speak again in a few days, once this has settled somewhat," he remarked before departing, leaving Mathew alone to process the weight of everything that had transpired.

Malcolm soon returned, this time to discuss a matter of delicate strategy. He explained that news of Mathew's existence, as the illegitimate child and heir to the throne of King Alexander, would not be announced through an official press release. Instead, the information would be selectively leaked to key members of the media. This, Malcolm assured him, was a calculated security measure.

"The press has an entire battalion of so-called 'royal watchers,'" Malcolm explained. "Their livelihoods depend on gathering intelligence about the royal family's movements, and any unexpected announcement, especially one as significant as yours, would blindside them. If they are caught completely unaware, they will scramble, intensify their efforts, and, in doing so, could pose a risk to security."

He leaned back slightly, studying Mathew's expression before continuing. "It is far safer to let them believe they've 'discovered' you through their own channels, rather than have them thrust into a frenzy by an official proclamation. By guiding the narrative subtly, we can control the pace of their response and ensure a smoother transition into your public role."

Mathew absorbed the information carefully. The sheer level of thought and precision behind even this one decision was staggering. It was becoming increasingly clear that nothing in the royal world happened by chance, it was all part of a carefully woven tapestry of strategy, security, and perception.

Before Mathew departed for his hotel, Blair Washington pulled him aside for a final briefing. In a measured, authoritative tone, the head of royal security outlined the next steps in Mathew's transition into the public eye.

"Before the official press release, you will be moved to a private residence," Blair explained. "This location will serve as both your temporary lodging and the venue for a series of full-day induction sessions. Over the coming days, you'll meet with key members of the royal household, undergo further briefings, and, of course, have additional discussions with the King himself."

He paused, ensuring Mathew was following before adding, "All of this is part of a carefully structured security strategy. The private residence will provide a controlled environment, one where you can prepare without the immediate scrutiny of the press or the public. Until your existence is formally acknowledged, our priority is to manage exposure and ensure that your introduction unfolds on our terms, not theirs."

Mathew nodded, absorbing the weight of Blair's words. Every move, every decision, was meticulously planned, a stark reminder that his life was no longer his own.

As Mathew stepped outside, he saw that his car had arrived to return him to his hotel, or so he thought. Amused, he watched as a total of four identical cars pulled up in succession. Three other men, all dressed in suits remarkably similar to his own, emerged from the building, each slipping into one of the waiting vehicles before they promptly pulled away. It was a carefully orchestrated manoeuvre, a decoy tactic designed to throw off anyone who might be watching.

Mathew entered the fourth car, and to his delight, he found Callum already inside, lounging comfortably with his usual air of casual mischief.

"Change of venue, old chap," Callum greeted him with a knowing smirk. "Your gear's already been sent to your new abode. Apparently, they're 'press leaking' this evening, and the paparazzi will be on the prowl."

He grinned as the car smoothly pulled away from the curb, merging seamlessly into the London traffic. The game had officially begun.

Callum glanced at Mathew, reading the tension in his face. "Do you want to talk? It's allowed, you know, up to you, really," he said, his voice reassuring.

Mathew exhaled sharply and sank back into the plush leather seat, running a hand through his hair. "I'm just so confused. Excited too, of course, but very, fucking, confused, I must say."

Without a word, Callum reached into his coat and produced a well-worn pewter drinking flask, handing it over with a subtle nod. "Bourbon and Coke," he muttered knowingly.

Mathew took it without hesitation, bringing the flask to his lips and taking three deep swigs, the warmth of the alcohol burning pleasantly down his throat. He sighed, already feeling the tension ease just slightly, then made to pass the flask back.

"You keep it, it's yours," Callum said with a grin, leaning back with an air of satisfaction.

Mathew turned the flask over in his hands, considering everything that had happened in the past twenty-four hours. He had stepped into a world of power, secrecy, and expectation, a world he barely understood. But for now, with Callum beside him and a drink in his hand, he allowed himself a rare moment of calm before the storm.

They arrived at Barkley Hall, one of the King's privately owned residences, an opulent estate that stood among the many grand homes he maintained across the British Isles, France, and Spain. It was a mansion in every sense of the word, exuding a level of elegance and history that no hotel could ever hope to match.

     Max Barrington

As the car came to a smooth stop, the grandeur of the estate became even more apparent. Towering stone columns framed the entrance, and soft golden light spilled from the vast arched windows, casting a warm glow over the manicured gardens. The sheer scale of the residence was imposing, yet there was an undeniable charm to it, an air of quiet authority, befitting the home of a king.

Upon entering the grand foyer, they were greeted by the concierge, a sharply dressed gentleman who welcomed them with a practiced grace. "Good evening, gentlemen," he said smoothly, inclining his head slightly. "Might I suggest a drink at the bar before you settle in?"

Callum, ever the connoisseur of good hospitality, gave an approving nod. "That sounds like an excellent idea," he said, glancing at Mathew, who silently agreed as they followed the concierge through the hall.

The bar was as refined as one would expect from a royal residence, more akin to the private lounges of a five-star hotel or the lavish interiors of a high-end casino. Dark mahogany paneling, gleaming brass fixtures, and plush leather seating set the tone for an evening of quiet luxury. A crystal chandelier overhead cast a soft, ambient glow, while an array of the finest spirits from around the world lined the polished bar.

They took their seats at a corner table, and within moments, a well-dressed attendant appeared, presenting them with their chosen drinks with the kind of seamless efficiency that spoke of years of refined service.

Mathew took a slow sip, letting the rich warmth of the bourbon settle, as Callum leaned back in his chair with an air of satisfaction. "Now this," he said with a smirk, swirling his glass, "Is how one should properly arrive at their new abode."

Callum leaned back in his chair, watching Mathew over the rim of his glass. "What was your impression of your father, the King, may I ask?" he inquired candidly, his tone light yet undeniably curious.

Mathew exhaled and ran a hand through his hair, considering the question. "I must admit," he said openly, "he seemed... very impersonal. Other than a handshake and a pat on the back, there wasn't much warmth. Is that how he treats his other children?"

Callum smirked knowingly and gestured for the steward to bring another round of drinks before responding. "The British royal children are often raised with a certain... distance. It's a combination of history, culture, and practicality." He swirled the amber liquid in his glass. "Historically, royal parents haven't exactly been hands-on. Nannies and governesses have traditionally done most of the raising, which inevitably leads to a sense of detachment."

Mathew listened intently, nodding slowly as he processed the information.

"And then," Callum continued, "there's the sheer weight of royal duty. The demands of the crown don't exactly allow for bedtime stories and Sunday picnics. Between official engagements, state visits, and everything in between, there's very little time left for parenting in the conventional sense." He lifted his glass in a half-toast before taking a sip.

Mathew sighed. "I suppose I never really looked at it that way," he admitted.

"There's also the matter of tradition and protocol," Callum added. "The royal family places enormous importance on decorum, and that extends to how children are raised. Public displays of affection? Practically unheard of. Warmth and informality? Kept strictly behind closed doors, if they exist at all." He arched a brow. "Not exactly the most nurturing environment, but it's the way it's always been."

Mathew took another sip of his drink, mulling over Callum's words.

"But enough of that," Callum said suddenly, clapping his hands together. "Would you like some supper? Perhaps a steak?"

Mathew blinked in surprise and let out a laugh. "A steak? My God, it's just after midnight. Where are we supposed to get a steak at this hour?"

Callum merely grinned and turned to the steward. "My friend will have a steak and so shall I," he said, then glanced back at Mathew. "How do you like it cooked?"

Mathew shook his head in amused disbelief. "Medium rare," he answered.

Callum nodded approvingly. "Excellent choice." Then, as if nothing was out of the ordinary, he lifted his glass once more. "Welcome to royal life, old chap. Here, midnight steaks are the least of the extravagances." He then said very quietly, "By the way, the staff here do not know who you are, not yet anyway."

The next morning at breakfast Callum passed the London Times to Mathew;

Secret Prince No More: Mathew to Be Welcomed as Heir

By Christian Pearson: London Daily

In a stunning revelation that has sent shockwaves through the monarchy, Buckingham Palace has confirmed that King Alexander's illegitimate son, Mathew, will be formally welcomed as heir to the throne. The unprecedented move marks a historic shift in royal tradition and raises questions about the future of the British monarchy.

For years, rumours of the King's secret son have circulated among royal watchers, but palace officials remained tight-lipped. Now, following a carefully orchestrated press leak, the existence of Mathew has been officially acknowledged, paving the way for his integration into royal life.

Sources close to the palace describe Mathew as a well-educated and charismatic man, reportedly in his early thirties, who has spent most of his life outside the public eye. His mother, whose identity has not been disclosed, is believed to have had a long-standing relationship with King Alexander before his ascension to the throne.

A spokesperson for the King issued a brief statement:
"His Majesty has long been aware of Mathew's existence, and after much consideration, he has decided to formally welcome him into the royal fold. The King is confident that Mathew will embrace his responsibilities with the dignity and commitment expected of a future heir."

Palace insiders indicate that Mathew has already begun intensive training on royal protocol, history, and state affairs under the guidance of key advisors. His public debut is expected in the coming weeks, with a series of carefully curated engagements designed to introduce him to the nation.

Public reaction has been mixed. While some see this as a progressive and modern step for the monarchy, others question the implications for the current line of succession. As of now, no official changes have been announced regarding other royals who were previously considered next in line.

Royal historian Dr. Eleanor Westbury commented on the significance of the moment:

"This is unprecedented in modern royal history. While illegitimate children of monarchs have existed throughout the ages, they were never formally recognised as heirs. King Alexander's decision signals a shift toward transparency and, perhaps, a break from rigid traditions."

With the world watching, Mathew's journey from private citizen to royal heir promises to be one of the most intriguing chapters in the monarchy's recent history. As he prepares to step into the spotlight, one question remains: will he be embraced by the people as their future king?

Having read the article Mathew returned it to the table and continued with his breakfast, "Seems that it is all about to start." He commented.

"I think it has well and truly commenced!" Added Callum, "I've been told to tell you that you have an appointment with the King at ten o'clock this morning, it's here on level one in his office…" and then added with a smirk "don't be late!" Just as the steward placed another newspaper down o the breakfast table. Mathew picked it up on opened it;

Prince Arnold Outraged Over Half-Brother's Claim to the Throne

By Suzanne Throng, The Daily Triumph.

The royal family is in turmoil following the shocking revelation that King Alexander's illegitimate son, Mathew, is to be welcomed as heir to the throne. Prince Arnold, long presumed to be the rightful successor, has expressed his fury at the decision, calling it a "disgraceful betrayal of royal tradition."

Sources close to the Prince report that he was blindsided by the announcement and had received no prior warning about his father's intentions. "Prince Arnold is in utter disbelief," an insider revealed. "He has dedicated his life to his role, upholding the monarchy's values and preparing for the duties that come with being the King's son. Now, all of that is being cast aside in favour of an outsider, someone who has never borne the weight of royal responsibility."

The Prince, known for his composed demeanour in public, is said to be "seething" behind palace walls, reportedly describing the move as "an insult to the Crown, the Constitution, and everything this family stands for." While he has yet to make an official statement, those close to him suggest that he is determined to challenge the decision.

"This isn't just about his personal feelings," a royal commentator explained. "This is about the very foundation of the monarchy. The notion that an illegitimate son, raised outside of the royal fold, could be inserted into the line of succession is deeply controversial. It sets a dangerous precedent."

Prince Arnold, who has served in the military and undertaken numerous royal engagements on behalf of his father, is widely seen as the natural successor. His supporters argue that Mathew, who has only recently been acknowledged by the King, lacks the experience and public trust necessary for such a role.

Public reaction has been divided, with some seeing the King's decision as a progressive step toward modernising the monarchy, while others echo Prince Arnold's concerns. Critics of the move argue that hereditary succession must remain unquestioned, and that recognising an illegitimate child undermines the monarchy's stability.

With tensions mounting behind palace doors, all eyes are now on Prince Arnold. Will he accept this decision, or will he fight for what he believes to be his rightful place as heir? One thing is certain, this royal storm is far from over.

The King's office, located on the first floor, was a striking blend of luxury and authority. It exuded an air of opulence while maintaining a distinctly business-like atmosphere. Rich mahogany paneling adorned the walls, complementing the deep green velvet drapes that framed the towering windows, which allowed streams of natural light to illuminate the room.

A massive antique desk, polished to perfection, stood at the heart of the office, its surface meticulously arranged with documents, a gilded fountain pen, and an ornate clock that quietly marked the passage of time. Behind it, an imposing high-backed leather chair added to the commanding presence of the space.

The decor was a seamless fusion of heritage and modern efficiency, framed portraits of past monarchs hung alongside state-of-the-art communication systems, ensuring that the room functioned as both a historical sanctuary and a fully operational nerve centre for royal affairs. Plush armchairs and a well-stocked sideboard hinted at more informal discussions, while towering bookshelves, lined with leather-bound volumes of law, diplomacy, and history, served as a silent reminder of the weight of the monarchy's responsibilities.

The King was visibly displeased, and it became immediately clear upon Mathew's arrival. Without a word of greeting, he handed Mathew a copy of the morning's newspaper, the bold headline emblazoned across the front page referring to Prince Arnold's scathing comments.

It wasn't the remarks themselves that troubled the King, he had expected resistance from Arnold, but rather the astonishing speed with which they had been delivered to the press. For Arnold's words to appear in print so swiftly, someone within the royal circle must have leaked the information, and that was what truly enraged him.

The King's expression was steely, his fingers tightening around the edges of the newspaper as he exhaled sharply. "This didn't happen by chance," he said, his tone controlled but laced with irritation.

"Someone within these walls had access to this information before it was meant to be public knowledge, and they wasted no time in feeding it to the press."

He paused, his piercing gaze settling on Mathew. "It's not a matter of what Arnold said, it's the principle of it. There's a breach in my own house, and that is unacceptable."

Mathew could sense the weight of the situation. This was no ordinary family dispute; this was a threat to the King's authority, and in the world of monarchy and power, perception was everything.

The King had composed himself somewhat, though a lingering intensity remained in his eyes. He fixed Mathew with a serious look and lowered his voice.

"What I'm about to tell you," he said gravely, "must remain in the strictest confidence."

Mathew nodded without hesitation. "Of course. You have my word."

Satisfied, the King leaned back in his chair and exhaled slowly before launching into an unbroken explanation that lasted nearly two hours. He spoke with the authority of a man who had deliberated over this matter for a long time, his words measured yet laced with undeniable conviction.

The crux of the issue, he revealed, was that he did not want his youngest son, Arnold, to inherit the throne. The King was blunt in his reasoning, making no effort to soften his stance. He openly stated that Arnold was a homosexual, something widely speculated upon but, to Mathew's knowledge, never officially acknowledged by the palace. The King's expression made it clear that, in his mind, the subject itself was not up for discussion.

However, Arnold's sexuality was not the sole concern. The true issue, the King explained, was Arnold's partner, Melvin Clarkson. The relationship between the two men had been no fleeting affair;

Arnold had married Melvin, a prospect the King found entirely disgusting and unacceptable and in effort to despite the King.

His jaw tightened as he continued. "It is not simply about personal choices, Mathew. This is about the monarchy, about duty, about the perception of the Crown. Arnold has always been reckless, and Melvin… well, Melvin is an opportunist."

Mathew remained silent, listening carefully as the King elaborated further, detailing the political ramifications, the concerns of advisors, and the undercurrents of discontent that such a union would stir within the establishment. This was not merely a family matter, nor was the crisis of succession the sole concern. According to King Alexander, the true danger lay in Melvin Clarkson himself. The King was convinced that Clarkson harboured destructive intentions, an insidious ambition that, if left unchecked, would see him drive a wedge through the heart of the royal family, alienating them from one another and destabilising the institution itself.

The King's expression darkened as he leaned forward, his voice carrying the weight of a man who had spent many sleepless nights wrestling with the implications of the situation. He told Mathew that he had already taken steps to explore an alternative course of action, one that would, in theory, undo the current line of succession.

He had formally raised the matter within Parliament, proposing to rescind his abdication and reassume the throne. It was, he admitted, a desperate measure, but one he had been willing to consider if it meant preserving the stability of the monarchy. However, after extensive consultations with constitutional experts and legal advisors, it had become painfully clear that the process would be neither swift nor favourable.

Even if Parliament agreed to take up the matter, it could take as long as eighteen months to reach a formal decision. And the outcome? The King was certain that the final ruling would not be in his favour. The precedent was too strong, the legal framework too rigid. The abdication had been final, and there was little appetite within the government, or the public, for that matter, to entertain such a reversal.

Mathew listened intently, absorbing the gravity of his father's words. The implications were undeniable. King Alexander had exhausted every conceivable avenue to prevent Arnold from taking the throne, and now, with his own reinstatement no longer a viable option, he was left with only one course of action: Mathew.

The King fixed Mathew with a steady, unwavering gaze, his expression a mixture of resolve and finality.

"You," he said, his voice firm yet measured, "will, at some stage today, after the inevitable fanfare and an excessive amount of ceremonial fuss, be officially named the rightful heir to the throne."

There was no hesitation in his words, no room for doubt. This was not a suggestion, nor was it a discussion. It was a declaration, absolute and unwavering.

"You shall not ascend to the throne until the matter before Parliament is resolved in the negative," the King continued, his tone measured but firm. "If, by some strange quirk of fate, it is resolved in the positive, then you shall remain heir apparent until my demise."

His words carried the weight of finality, leaving no room for interpretation. This was the course that had been set, and Mathew was now firmly within its grasp.

"I will expect your unwavering loyalty, no matter which way the good Lord chooses to let this course unfold," the King said, his voice resolute. "And more than that, I expect your steadfast allegiance in ensuring that Prince Arnold does not hasten his path to the throne."

The gravity of the moment hung between them as the King extended his hand toward Mathew. Without hesitation, Mathew grasped it firmly, meeting his father's gaze with unwavering determination.

"You have my word," he said, his tone carrying the weight of full agreement.

"I shall present you to Parliament tomorrow morning," the King declared, his tone leaving no room for debate. "You will wear your Australian Army Ceremonial Dress uniform of a Lieutenant Colonel. It will be delivered to you later today."

Mathew blinked, momentarily taken aback. A Lieutenant Colonel? He had never attained that rank. In fact, he had left the army years ago. But something in the King's unwavering expression made it clear that now was not the time to question details. Perhaps, he reasoned, it was best to let this particular matter slide, for now.

Heir Apparent: HRH Prince Mathew

Address by King Alexander IV to the Parliament of England
On the Presentation of HRH Prince Mathew as Heir Apparent

Honourable Members of Parliament,
My Lords, Ladies and Gentlemen,

It is with great gravity and a profound sense of duty that I stand before you today to address a matter of the utmost national significance, one that speaks to the continuity of the Crown, the stability of our great nation, and the steadfast traditions that have guided us for centuries.

As you are all aware, the question of succession has, in recent months, been the subject of much discussion both within these halls and beyond. The sacred duty of the monarchy is not only to serve but to ensure the enduring strength and stability of the realm. It is in light of this responsibility that I come before you today to present to you His Royal Highness, Prince Mathew, a son of the House of Wynasleigh and now heir apparent to the throne of England.

This decision has not been made lightly, nor has it been taken without deep reflection on what is best for the future of this nation. Prince Mathew, by virtue of his lineage, his character, and his unwavering commitment to duty, stands ready to shoulder the burden that comes with sovereignty. Though his journey to this position has been unconventional, let there be no doubt that his right to stand as heir to the throne is resolute and undisputed.

Prince Mathew has spent his life in service to the ideals we hold dear, strength, honour, and devotion to country. As a decorated officer of the Australian Army, he has demonstrated leadership, courage, and a resolute commitment to duty. He has walked the path of honour not by birthright alone, but by his actions and his unwavering dedication to the principles of service.

As heir apparent, he will undergo the necessary preparation to assume the weighty responsibilities that accompany the Crown. Under my guidance and that of this esteemed institution, he shall be afforded the knowledge and counsel necessary to lead with wisdom, justice, and unwavering integrity.

I ask you now, honourable members of Parliament, to recognise Prince Mathew in his rightful place as the heir to the throne. Let his presence here today serve as a testament to the unwavering endurance of our monarchy and our shared commitment to upholding the traditions that have long been the foundation of this great nation.

Together, let us move forward with strength and unity, ensuring that our beloved England remains a beacon of stability and prosperity for generations to come.

God Save the King.

Response of the Parliament of England

It is with due reverence and deep consideration that this esteemed body acknowledges the address you have delivered today. The question of succession is, as you have rightly stated, one of paramount importance, for it determines not only the future of the monarchy but the continued stability of our nation.

Parliament recognises the gravity of your declaration and extends its solemn duty in deliberating upon the appointment of **HRH** Prince Mathew as heir apparent. His lineage, character, and service to the Commonwealth have been presented with clarity, and while this Parliament respects Your Majesty's judgement, we also acknowledge the unprecedented nature of this decision.

The constitutional framework upon which our great nation stands must guide us, and as such, this matter shall be discussed and reviewed with the utmost diligence. The traditions and laws that have safeguarded the monarchy for generations must be upheld, ensuring that any transition in the line of succession is executed with the full confidence of this governing body and the people it represents.

Your Majesty, the loyalty of Parliament to the Crown remains steadfast, as does our commitment to ensuring that the monarchy continues to be a pillar of strength and unity. We shall convene in the coming days to deliberate further on this historic development, seeking to uphold the principles of governance, duty, and national stability. May wisdom guide us, and may the unity of our great nation endure.

God Save the King.

And just like that, it was done, bar the applause. Mathew was now, officially and irrevocably, the heir to the throne of England. The weight of history settled upon him, yet the moment itself had passed with surprising swiftness. No grand ceremony, no thunderous ovation, just the quiet finality of an unspoken truth.

Max Barrington

As the car pulled away from Parliament House, Callum turned to him with a proud smile. "Congratulations, Your Highness," he said, his voice warm with admiration. Mathew managed a small nod, still processing the gravity of what had just transpired.

His attention shifted to the decoy convoy peeling away from the underground secure car park. Several vehicles, indistinguishable from the one he sat in, were departing in different directions, each carrying Australian Army Lieutenant Colonels as part of an elaborate security operation. The level of precaution was staggering.

He watched in quiet astonishment as the convoy executed its well-rehearsed deception, all designed to obscure his true whereabouts. The sheer scale of the effort left him both humbled and uneasy. Was this his new reality? A life of secrecy, of calculated misdirection, where even his movements were shrouded in layers of protection?

Within the safety and security of the car, Mathew turned to Callum, his voice low with cautious urgency. "Is it safe to speak in here? There's something the King told me earlier that I need to discuss."

Callum, ever composed, offered a reassuring nod. "Absolutely. This vehicle is equipped with a sophisticated counter-surveillance system. It constantly transmits bogus communications to hundreds of random addresses every minute, rendering any bugging devices, inside or outside, completely useless." He paused, then added with a knowing smile, "So, I'm all ears, old chap."

Mathew hesitated for a moment, his expression betraying a flicker of doubt. Callum noticed it immediately and leaned in slightly, his tone shifting to one of quiet sincerity.

"You'll need someone to confide in, Mathew. Someone you can trust, impeccably and without question. Under normal circumstances, that kind of trust takes years to build. Unfortunately, you don't have the luxury of time. What I'm trying to say is… you can trust me. You can treat me as your confidant."

Mathew exhaled slowly, absorbing Callum's words. "I want to trust you, Callum," he admitted. "And I don't mean to seem doubtful, it's just as you said, trust usually takes time. But… yes. I do trust you."

A sense of relief settled over him. The weight on his shoulders felt just a little lighter. Feeling more at ease, Mathew sat back and let out a deep breath before turning to Callum once more. "The King believes there is a leak within his personal staff," he confided.

Callum's reaction was immediate; his face darkened with shock. "A leak? You mean someone close to him is feeding information outside?" His mind raced, but before he could say more, a realisation struck him. "I'll bet it has something to do with the timing of Arnie's reply in the press."

Mathew nodded, his eyes narrowing. "I think you're right, mate. It was when he handed me the paper with Arnie's comments that the King brought it up."

Callum registered Mathew's words with a subtle shift in expression. The use of 'mate', so casual yet significant, was not lost on him. And referring to Prince Arnold as 'Arnie', that was a deliberate signal. It was Mathew's way of telling him, without explicitly stating it, that he had been accepted into his circle of trust.

After a moment of contemplation, Callum spoke again, his tone measured yet eager. "The man in charge of internal security, Blair Washington, is a good mate of mine. He's also a naval officer and one of the most meticulous men I know when it comes to security. What do you think about inviting him to dinner tonight? Just something casual, the three of us."

Mathew considered the suggestion, sensing the weight behind it. Callum clearly trusted Blair, and given the gravity of their discussion, it might be a wise move.

Callum continued, reading Mathew's expression. "It would give you some real insight into just how pedantic the house is about security.

Blair has firsthand experience dealing with these kinds of concerns."

Mathew finally nodded. "Yes, I have already met Blair and had a session on internal security with him, he does seem to be a knowledgable sort of chap. Alright. Let's do it."

Blair Washington, the head of internal security for the House of the Monarch, is a seasoned naval officer with an unyielding commitment to duty. A man of imposing presence, he carries himself with the quiet confidence of someone who has spent years navigating high-stakes operations. His sharp blue eyes miss nothing, and his salt-and-pepper hair, always neatly trimmed, adds to his air of authority.

Blair's reputation is built on his meticulous attention to detail and an almost obsessive approach to security. He is methodical, calculated, and entirely unsentimental when it comes to his work. Those who know him understand that his loyalty is absolute, he serves the Crown with unwavering devotion, and he expects the same from those under his command.

Despite his rigid professionalism, Blair is not without charm. In private settings, he has a dry wit and a sharp mind, qualities that make him an engaging conversationalist when he chooses to be. He and Callum share a long-standing friendship, forged through years of mutual respect and collaboration.

Blair's experience in counter intelligence has made him a master of deception, surveillance, and crisis management. If there is a leak within the King's inner circle, Blair Washington is precisely the kind of man who will find it, and eliminate it.

Blair held the esteemed position of Commander within the Navy Security Service (NSS), a branch of the Royal Navy that specialises in safeguarding naval operations and intelligence. The NSS is known for its close collaboration with MI5 and MI6, Britain's domestic and foreign intelligence agencies, respectively, ensuring a seamless integration of security efforts across military and national intelligence frameworks.

The dinner that followed was a delightfully informal affair, thoroughly enjoyed by all three attendees. The meal, thoughtfully suggested and highly recommended by the head steward, featured roast beef accompanied by horseradish sauce, a dish deeply rooted in the tradition of the House Cavalry. This culinary choice was not

		Max Barrington

only a nod to the storied history of the cavalry but also a testament to the expertise of one of the resident chefs, who had mastered the art of preparing this iconic dish.

The evening unfolded as a seamless fusion of camaraderie, tradition, and exceptional cuisine, creating an atmosphere that lingered long after the last bite. Conversations flowed effortlessly, and the warmth of the gathering left an indelible mark on all who attended. As the group transitioned into the bar lounge, they ordered fresh drinks from the attentive steward, further sinking into a state of relaxation. Blair, with an air of openness, was more than willing to indulge Mathew's curiosity, offering insightful responses to his questions about the meticulous measures taken to ensure both secrecy and privacy when it came to protecting an individual's identity.

Mathew was particularly captivated when Blair delved into the intricacies of maintaining absolute privacy within the residence. Blair explained how seemingly trivial details, like photographs taken of individuals in this setting, could inadvertently expose sensitive information. He emphasised that the simple act of leaving the background untouched, whether it be a distinctive wallpaper pattern or a carefully placed object, could provide a crucial clue to the location. For example, the unique design of the wallpaper might be traced back to its origin, and from there, the specific place where it had been installed could be deduced. Similarly, objects such as vases or works of art, though seemingly innocuous, could be identified through their distinct features or provenance, and tracking their current locations could ultimately lead to the discovery of the residence's whereabouts. It was a reminder of how every detail, no matter how small, could be a potential thread in unravelling the larger tapestry of secrecy.

Mathew was thoroughly impressed and couldn't help but inquire about the fleet of vehicles and their look-alike occupants, wondering how they contributed to the decoy service. Blair chuckled, clearly enjoying the curiosity, and explained that the operation was far more complex than it appeared. He revealed that in order to prevent any royal or house vehicle from being linked to a specific residence or office, every single vehicle in the fleet was registered to the London Police at New Scotland Yard, London W1. This clever measure ensured that no one could trace the vehicles back to a particular location. To further enhance the illusion, the individuals driving the cars were all police officers, each possessing advanced driver certification, skilled in evasive manoeuvres and high-speed driving techniques. Meanwhile, the passengers in the vehicles were members of the Household Cavalry, adding yet another layer of authenticity to the decoy operation. It was an intricate and well co-ordinated system, designed to preserve privacy and maintain an air of plausible deniability, leaving Mathew in awe of the meticulous planning that went into such operations.

After another round of drinks, the conversation turned to the tragic events at the snowfields. Mathew, who knew little about the incident beyond what he had read in a local Australian paper, listened intently as Blair and Callum both expressed their disgust with the inquiry into what had happened on the mountain.

Mathew, unaware of the details, casually asked, "I thought it was an avalanche? An accident." He had assumed it was just a natural disaster, something that couldn't be avoided.

Blair's expression soured as he shook his head. "In this day and age, we have systems in place to prevent avalanches or at the very least, to provide fair warning," he said, his voice tinged with frustration. "I think the investigation into its cause has been absolutely piss-poor. It's hard to believe that such a tragedy could have happened with the technology and precautions we have now."

He went on to explain that avalanche conditions are continuously monitored by highly trained personnel, backed by sophisticated electronic equipment designed to predict and prevent such disasters. "These systems rarely fail," Blair added with conviction.

Callum, who had been quietly listening, suddenly interjected. "But... it did fail, didn't it?" His question hung in the air, a subtle

      Max Barrington

but pointed reminder that despite the advanced technology, something had gone terribly wrong. Mathew, still trying to piece everything together, sensed the gravity of the situation, realising that the tragedy was far from a simple accident.

"I can see so many areas that were just completely overlooked; it's ridiculous, criminal really," Blair said with confidence. "I would've run the investigation and inquiry completely differently, there's so much they missed."

Mathew, who had been listening intently, casually asked, "Why don't you then?" as he walked over to the bar to grab the next round, momentarily putting the steward in a bit of a dilemma. It wasn't often that guests took it upon themselves to fetch their own drinks, but Mathew seemed unfazed by the unspoken rules of service.

Blair accepted his drink from Mathew with a nod of thanks before responding, "The officer in charge of external security audits, Commander Hugh Drinkwater, won't let me take part in the investigation."

"Does he outrank you?" Mathew asked, his tone easy, almost offhand, as he took a sip of his drink.

"No, we're the same rank, both commanders. He just happens to be in charge of external, and that's the end of it," Blair replied, his voice firm, as if that were the final word on the matter.

Mathew's gaze flicked to Callum, who leaned back in his chair, looking completely at ease. With a smirk, Callum asked, "What if Mat promoted you and gave you a warrant to conduct an investigation? Would that fix things?" His tone was light, almost playful, as if he were merely tossing out the idea for amusement.

Blair, who had been lounging comfortably, suddenly straightened, his eyes locking onto Mathew with newfound intensity. "Would you?" he asked, his voice now carrying a weight that shifted the entire mood of the conversation.

Mathew didn't hesitate. "Of course I will. If you have even the slightest suspicion about King Albert's death, then it needs to be looked into. No matter how small or insignificant something may seem, every lead, every irregularity should be investigated. And I, for one, am all for it." He drained the last of his drink and stretched slightly before adding, "I'll speak to the King about it in the morning. Speaking of which, I'm seeing him at ten-thirty, so I'd better think about calling it a night."

With that, Mathew stood up and began heading towards his rooms.

"I'll pull the bed down for you!" Callum suddenly remembered his role and sprang to his feet, moving to follow.

"Fuck off, Callum!" Mathew laughed over his shoulder as he disappeared through the lounge entry. "Talk to you lot in the morning. We'll do lunch?"

As he made his way to his quarters, Mathew couldn't help but smile to himself. He was really starting to enjoy this new lifestyle, especially now that he was beginning to make real friends.

"Good morning… Prince Mathew," called out a now familiar voice, warm yet regal in tone. Mathew, standing at the breakfast buffet and in the midst of getting himself a coffee, turned to see none other than the King himself seated at the dining table. A steward was carefully placing a plate of Eggs Benedict before him, the rich aroma of hollandaise sauce filling the air.

"I do hope you don't mind me joining you for breakfast without notice," the King said smoothly, his expression calm yet keenly observant.

As Mathew reached for the coffee machine, a steward swiftly appeared at his side, ready to take over. But Mathew, not one for unnecessary formalities, waved him away with a casual gesture. "I've got it, thanks," he said, before adding, "I think I'll try the Eggs Benedict as well."

With his coffee in hand, he made his way toward the table where the King sat. "Good morning, sir," he greeted respectfully, gesturing toward the chair opposite as he waited for permission to join.

The King, mid-sip of his tea, gave a brief nod of approval. Mathew took his seat, settling in as the steward returned with his breakfast. As he picked up his cutlery, he couldn't help but wonder, was this just a casual thing, or was there something more to this unannounced breakfast meeting?

"It was weighing rather heavily on my mind last night," the King began, his tone measured yet laced with underlying tension. He set down his cup of tea, his gaze distant for a moment before refocusing on Mathew. "There are two major issues currently before Parliament that concern me deeply. And it suddenly became clear to me that if, " he paused, as if carefully considering his words, "and I do believe it could go either way, but if Parliament's decisions on both matters were to result in the negative…"

He drew in a slow breath, then leaned forward slightly, locking eyes with Mathew. His voice dropped, carrying a weight of unshakable resolve. "Then Arnold would inherit the throne."

A beat of silence hung between them, the gravity of the statement settling in the air. The King's expression hardened, his usual composed demeanour giving way to something far more personal, more urgent.

"I will not let that happen," he stated, his voice quiet yet unwavering. "I don't quite know how… but I will not let it happen."

Mathew could see the sheer determination in the King's eyes, this wasn't just a matter of duty or protocol. This was something deeper, something that struck at the very core of the monarchy itself.

"Do you have a contingency plan, sir?" Mathew asked, his curiosity piqued.

The King exhaled slowly, his fingers tapping lightly against the edge of his teacup. "That is precisely what I need," he admitted, his voice carrying the weight of the dilemma. "And no… I do not have one." He paused for a moment before continuing, his tone more deliberate. "That is part of the reason I wanted to speak with you about this."

His piercing gaze locked onto Mathew, his expression expectant. "I was rather hoping that with your, brilliant, so I have heard, legal background, you might be able to identify some form of contingency plan. Or, at the very least, assist in crafting one."

Mathew studied the King carefully. There was no idle flattery in his words, no attempt at courtly charm, just a direct appeal, a recognition of necessity. The weight of responsibility was clearly pressing on him, and now, that weight was being shared.

To Mathew, it seemed like an extraordinary coincidence that last night's discussion with Callum and Blair had raised strong suspicions about the avalanche, suggesting that it might not have been entirely a natural occurrence. The timing of it all felt almost too convenient, as though pieces of a much larger puzzle were beginning to fall into place.

A sudden and impulsive thought struck him, one that sent a spark of intrigue coursing through his mind. Without hesitation, he leaned forward slightly, formulating a response that he suspected might prove very interesting indeed.

"If… and I acknowledge it's only a very slight possibility," Mathew began carefully, his tone measured, "but if the avalanche could have been avoided, and if Arnold…" He hesitated briefly, his eyes searching the King's face before continuing with deliberate precision. "And here, I mean no offence… but if Arnold was, in some way, complicit in the terrible accident… then surely, he would lose all claim to the throne, would he not?"

Mathew let the question hang in the air, watching intently for the King's reaction. The implications of such a revelation were staggering. If there was even the faintest possibility that foul play had been involved, then not only would the monarchy's future be altered, but so too would the course of history itself.

The King's gaze locked onto Mathew, his expression unreadable. For a moment, time seemed to stretch, what felt like long, drawn-out seconds were, in reality, only fleeting milliseconds. Yet, in that brief moment, an unspoken intensity passed between them. Then, in a voice barely above a whisper, yet unmistakably firm, the King spoke, his eyes never wavering.

"That thought was at the back of my mind on that tragic day," he admitted, his tone laced with something between regret and quiet torment. "I hated myself for even considering it and dismissed it instantly… and now, you bring those very same thoughts back to the surface."

He paused, studying Mathew with renewed scrutiny before continuing, his voice low but deliberate. "Do you have some knowledge or information that led you to make such a comment?"

There was no accusation in his tone, but rather a deep, measured curiosity, perhaps even hope. Mathew could sense it. The King was not just asking a question; he was searching for something.

"I suppose I blame it on my legal training," Mathew said thoughtfully, swirling the last remnants of his coffee before setting the cup down. "I don't just question things that catch my attention, I scrutinise them, especially when something doesn't sit right with me." He paused briefly, choosing his words with care. "Now, I'll admit, I know nothing about avalanches. But I would liken it to a dam failure. If a modern dam were to collapse, one situated in a location where its failure would lead to catastrophe, including loss of life, there would be warning signs. Whether detected by human observation or electronic monitoring, some kind of alarm would be triggered."

He leaned back slightly, his gaze steady. "And a failure like that doesn't just happen out of nowhere. There's always a cause. A buildup of pressure, structural damage, environmental factors, something initiates the chain of events. And that 'something' is usually a process that unfolds over time, not an instantaneous, unexplained disaster."

Mathew finished his coffee and gestured to the steward for another, sensing that he might need it. His mind was already racing ahead, connecting thoughts, examining possibilities.

"I'd like to scrutinise the investigation that was conducted after the avalanche," he stated firmly, his tone leaving no room for doubt.

Mathew had the King's full attention. He had barely finished explaining his reasoning when the King suddenly sat forward, his eyes alight with a new intensity.

"Do it! My God, yes, what a brilliant idea!" The King's voice carried a surge of energy, as if Mathew had just unlocked a door he hadn't realised was there. "As far as I know, the investigation was handled solely by the Cantonal Police and the Sûreté of Switzerland. I don't believe it's ever been reviewed by our own people." He paused for the briefest moment before nodding, his decision made. "Yes! Do it. It certainly can't do any harm."

But then, as if catching himself, the King exhaled and shook his head. "That being said... I very much doubt Arnold had anything

                    Max Barrington

to do with it. In fact, I'd say, without hesitation, that he most definitely would never even consider such a thing!"

And yet, despite the firm declaration, there was something in the King's eyes, something hesitant, uncertain. A flicker of doubt that betrayed his words.

"I'll need some of our security fellows," Mathew added, sensing that now was the perfect moment to bring Blair Watson into the fold.

The King, who had just risen from the table, waved a hand in a gesture of approval. "Use whoever you think you'll need," he said without hesitation. "See Colonel Pundesh, he's head of staff. He'll provide you with the necessary staff warrants and any documentation required to gain access to the Swiss authorities."

As he moved toward the dining room entrance, he paused briefly, turning back to Mathew with a pointed look. "And don't forget our ten-thirty meeting in my office," he reminded him before disappearing through the doorway, leaving Mathew with much to consider.

Melvin Clarkson

Mathew had nearly an hour before his scheduled meeting with King Alex, and with some time to prepare, he settled at the desk in his accommodation rooms. The space had been set up for his use, and as he rifled through a drawer, he came across an internal telephone directory. He had just started scanning the list when the door opened, and Callum entered, looking decidedly worse for wear.

"My God! Look at you!" Mathew exclaimed, barely able to hide his amusement. Callum, usually so composed, appeared to be suffering from a severe hangover, his face pale, his eyes bloodshot, and his movements sluggish.

"I think you should be taking the day off, old son," Mathew added with a smirk, leaning back in his chair.

Callum groaned as he all but collapsed into the visitor's chair opposite the desk. "I believe the coffee I made earlier may have… malfunctioned," he muttered, rubbing his temples. "But I am certain that once I've had a second cup, I shall be just fine." He exhaled slowly, then gestured weakly toward the telephone directory in Mathew's hands. "Are you looking for someone?"

Mathew gave Callum a concise rundown of his earlier conversation with the King, outlining the key points of their discussion and the task ahead. As he flipped through the internal telephone directory, he explained that he was searching for Colonel Pundesh's contact details.

Callum, still looking a little worse for wear but clearly regaining some clarity, leaned forward slightly. "Before you ring Pundesh, I reckon you should have a word with Blair first," he suggested. "He'll have a better idea of what we're walking into and might even have some useful contacts in Switzerland."

Mathew considered this for a moment, then nodded. It made sense to get Blair involved as soon as possible.

"Oh, and about lunch," Callum continued, perking up slightly at the thought. "I've lined up a spot at the golf club just down the road. They put on a superb meal. Blair's already sorting out transport, but MI5 aren't too thrilled about the location, apparently, they're not keen on securing such a large, open area."

Mathew smirked. "I imagine they wouldn't be."

He nodded in agreement with the lunch plans as he gathered his notes and prepared to head off. "Right then, I'd better get moving, King Alex is expecting me."

As Mathew left for his meeting, Callum leaned back in his chair, rubbing his temples and muttering, "Might need a bloody third coffee at this rate."

One of the doormen stationed at the entrance to the King's office stepped forward as Mathew approached. "Please wait here, Your Highness," he said politely, before disappearing into the office to announce Mathew's arrival. The second doorman remained outside with him, standing at attention.

Moments later, the first doorman reappeared, nodding formally. "The King will see you now, Your Highness," he said, before stepping aside and leading Mathew through the grand double doors.

As Mathew entered, he was momentarily taken aback. He had expected to find King Alex alone, but instead, there was a woman seated in one of the four visitor chairs in front of the King's large desk. The King, noticing his reaction, gestured toward her with an air of casual authority.

"Mathew, allow me to introduce Her Majesty, Queen Charmaine."

Mathew, caught off guard by the unexpected introduction, quickly gathered himself. He bowed respectfully and addressed her by her proper title before standing motionless, uncertain of the protocol in this moment.

The King chuckled. "Please, sit down, Mathew. You're making the room feel unbalanced by just standing there." He turned to the

Queen with an affectionate smirk. "This is, obviously, my boy, Mathew."

The Queen regarded him with an amused but composed expression. "I can tell by his handsome looks, Alex," she said warmly before turning her full attention to Mathew. "Hello, Mathew. Please, relax and take a seat. I'm not going to bite you."

She smiled kindly as Mathew hesitated for only a second before lowering himself into a chair opposite her.

The Queen continued, her voice composed but carrying an unmistakable weight. "I understand you may be delving into the accident, the avalanche." She regarded Mathew steadily, her posture regal yet open. "If you think, even for a moment, that Arnold may have been involved, then you are most certainly on the wrong track. Pursuing such a notion would be a waste of time and, our, resources."

Her words were firm, but not unkind, and Mathew listened intently as she continued. "Contrary to some of the more malicious whispers that tend to circulate in certain circles, Arnold would never have harmed his brother, nor his wife, nor their children. I would consider it utterly despicable for anyone to even suggest such a thing about that boy."

She exhaled softly, a flicker of something unreadable passing through her expression. "Arnold has been a great disappointment to both the King and me in many ways… I think you already understand what I mean." She paused, waiting for Mathew's subtle nod of acknowledgment before continuing.

"If there was any foul play from that direction," she went on, her voice dropping slightly, "then I would suggest looking not at Arnold, but at Melvin Clarkson." A hint of revulsion crossed her features as she spoke the name. "Even saying it aloud disgusts me. There." She straightened slightly, smoothing a hand over the elegant fabric of her dress. "I have said what I wished to say."

The room fell silent for a moment, the air thick with the weight of her words. Mathew knew that this was not just a personal opinion, this was a carefully considered statement from a woman who had spent a lifetime observing the intricate and often treacherous world of royal politics. Mathew made a quiet but firm decision in that moment, Queen Charmaine was someone he would keep as an ally, a friend if possible, but never an adversary. To cross her, intentionally or otherwise, would be a grave mistake, one that could prove detrimental in ways he could not yet fully anticipate.

There was an undeniable strength beneath her composed exterior, a quiet authority that came not just from her title but from her lifetime of learning the complexities of court politics. She had chosen to speak candidly with him, and that in itself was significant. It was a gesture he would not take lightly.

Mathew knew that earning her trust would be valuable, but more importantly, he knew that losing it would be unforgivable.

As Queen Charmaine rose gracefully from her seat, both the King and Mathew instinctively followed suit, standing as a mark of respect. There was a regal air about her movements, a quiet authority that commanded attention without the need for words.

Pausing just before reaching the door, she turned slightly, her gaze settling on Mathew with an intensity that left no room for ambiguity. "I expect you to keep me informed of your inquiry," she said, her voice measured but firm. Then, with deliberate emphasis, she added, "Personally."

The weight of her request, or rather, her command, was not lost on Mathew. It was not a mere courtesy she was asking for, but a direct line of communication, bypassing any intermediaries. He inclined his head respectfully. "Of course, Your Majesty. You have my word."

Seemingly satisfied, the Queen gave a slight nod and exited the room, leaving behind a silence that felt heavier than before. Mathew exhaled slowly, his mind already turning over the implications of her request. This investigation was becoming more intricate by the minute.

The King had regained his seat and said to Mathew "That Clarkson is a total fool of a person, I refrain from calling him a man and really the word person is too good for the likes of him." Mathew had also resumed his seat and now looked at the King with interest. "How so?" Mathew simply asked.

The King sighed, leaning back in his chair as if suddenly weighed down by years of frustration. "Melvin Clarkson is… how shall I put this? A cancer within our family. He married into it, but unlike most who take on the responsibilities and traditions with a degree of respect, he exploited it from the moment he slipped the ring onto his finger."

Mathew folded his arms, listening intently.

"He is ambitious, conniving, and utterly self-serving. The man has no loyalty beyond his own desires. He came from a relatively privileged background, but that was never enough for him. Marrying into the royal family gave him a platform, one he used not to support the monarchy but to elevate himself. Every opportunity, every event, every speech, it was all about him, about how he had been 'trapped' by royal protocol, how he was a 'moderniser' being held back by outdated traditions."

Mathew nodded. "The way you describe him… he seems cut from some bad cloth. Someone who marries into royalty, enjoys the wealth, the influence, the prestige, but then complains endlessly about the supposed restrictions. Painting himself as a victim while simultaneously using the very institution he claims to despise for personal gain."

"Precisely," the King agreed. "Melvin and Arnold were once quite close, thick as thieves, you might say. But over time, even Arnold grew weary of him. Melvin is the sort of man who befriends people for their usefulness, not out of any genuine affection. When Arnold was at his strongest politically, Melvin was at his side, whispering in his ear, fanning the flames of his ambitions. But when Arnold's

                                    Max Barrington

influence began to wane, Melvin distanced himself and aligned with other figures who could serve his interests better."

Mathew exhaled sharply. "And now the Queen suspects that if anyone had a hand in the avalanche, it would be him?"

The King nodded grimly. "She would never say it outright, but she wouldn't have brought up his name if she didn't have strong suspicions. And frankly, I wouldn't put it past him. He has a way of staying just clear of direct involvement in anything scandalous, yet every time something disastrous happens, he always seems to be lurking nearby, untouched, ready to spin the narrative to his advantage."

Mathew sat back in his chair, absorbing everything. "Well, that certainly gives me another angle to consider."

The King smiled faintly, though there was little warmth in it. "Yes. And consider this, if Melvin Clarkson is truly involved, exposing him might serve more than just justice. It might finally rid us of a dangerous influence that has been poisoning this family for far too long."

He paused, his expression darkening, his voice lowering to a more somber tone. "But Mathew, a word of caution, watch your back." His eyes locked onto Mathew's with an intensity that made it clear this was not just a passing remark, but a genuine warning. "I have no doubt that our security is among the best in the world, and I trust our people implicitly. But I also know that Clarkson is no fool. He's had years to learn our systems, to identify weaknesses, to manipulate those who could serve his interests. He's not the type to get his own hands dirty, he's far too clever for that, but that doesn't mean he won't orchestrate something from the shadows."

Mathew absorbed the weight of the King's words. He had already begun to sense the depth of the intrigue surrounding the royal family, but hearing this from Alex himself made it all the more real. Melvin Clarkson wasn't just an opportunist, he was a threat.

"I appreciate the warning," Mathew said, his voice steady. "And I'll take every precaution necessary. But if he's involved, I won't stop until I have proof."

The King studied him for a long moment before nodding. "Good. Just be smart about it. He plays a long game, Mathew, and if you're not careful, you may find yourself a pawn on his board before you even realise it."

Mathew gave a small, confident smirk. "Then I suppose it's time to change the game," he said, locking eyes with the King as a wry smile spread across his lips.

The King chuckled, shaking his head slightly. "Indeed," he murmured, before straightening in his chair. "But for now, you'd better get along to your luncheon at the club. I expect the others are anxiously waiting for you."

Mathew's expression shifted to one of mild astonishment. He hadn't mentioned the lunch to the King, at least, not directly.

Alex caught the look and grinned knowingly. "Come now, Mathew," he said, amusement lacing his voice. "I am the King. I make it my business to know what's happening in my own house. Well... at least when it comes to matters as significant as lunchtime gatherings."

Mathew let out a small chuckle, shaking his head in admiration at the King's ever-present awareness.

"I would join you," Alex continued, rising from his chair with an air of finality, "but I have another meeting to attend. So go, enjoy yourself. And do try to eat something. You'll need your strength."

With a final nod of respect, Mathew turned and made his way toward the exit. As he stepped through the doors, he couldn't help but feel the weight of the conversation still lingering in his mind. The game was changing indeed, and he intended to make sure he was the one setting the rules.

On his way back to his rooms to get changed and find Callum, Mathew's mobile phone rang. He frowned slightly, only two people had this number: his mother and his girlfriend.

A quick glance at the screen confirmed it was Rhianna. His stomach dropped. Rhianna. He had completely forgotten about her. In fact, he had forgotten about everything back in Australia.

Things in Britain had been a whirlwind, so much had happened in such a short time that his personal life had taken a complete backseat. Now, a wave of guilt washed over him. He had promised Rhianna he would call as soon as he arrived. That was three days ago.

He hesitated a moment before answering, bracing himself.

"Oh... is that you, Mathew?" came Rhianna's voice, dripping with icy sarcasm. "Are you still alive, Mathew? Did you forget to call me? Well… fuck you!"

The line went dead.

Mathew exhaled sharply, running a hand through his hair. He was about to call her back when Callum's voice cut through his thoughts.

"The car's waiting!"

Mathew glanced at his watch. There was no time for damage control now. I'll call her back tonight, he told himself.

But he didn't.

By the time the evening rolled around, the day had drained him. One drink led to another, one conversation bled into the next, and by the time his head hit the pillow, he was out like a light.

And Rhianna? Forgotten once again.

Dossier on Melvin Clarkson

It was to be a think tank morning in respect to where, and how, to commence their investigation, they each had a dossier on Melvin Clarkson.

Name: Melvin Jonathan Clarkson
Date of Birth: April 3, 1972
Nationality: British

Born into a family of old money with aristocratic ties, Melvin Clarkson enjoyed a privileged upbringing. Educated at Eton and later Oxford, where he studied Political Science and Economics, he was known for his intelligence and ruthless ambition. Even in his university years, Clarkson demonstrated a Machiavellian approach to personal and professional relationships, often manoeuvring people to his advantage while maintaining an affable public image.

Clarkson's early career saw him working in finance, where he quickly built a reputation for being cutthroat. He amassed a fortune through a series of aggressive corporate takeovers, some of which led to allegations of insider trading, though no charges were ever proven.

Leveraging his wealth, Clarkson transitioned into political circles, offering generous donations to various parties and forming close ties with influential figures. His ability to manipulate the media and control narratives made him a dangerous asset to those in power and a feared opponent to those who crossed him.

Clarkson's ties to the monarchy began subtly, attending high-profile events and ingratiating himself with key figures. Over time, he became particularly close to Prince Arnold, a known associate of Clarkson in social and business dealings. This connection, however, raised concerns among the monarchy and government officials, as Clarkson's reputation for underhanded tactics was well established.

His relationship with Arnold fuelled speculation that he sought to use the prince as a pawn for his own political and financial interests. Rumours of Clarkson attempting to influence decisions within the

Max Barrington

royal court led to tension between him and the reigning monarch, King Alex.

Clarkson's name has been linked to several political and financial scandals, but his most infamous suspected involvement is in the tragic avalanche that claimed the life of the Crown Prince. While no concrete evidence has surfaced, whispers in elite circles suggest Clarkson may have played a role, whether through direct orchestration or indirect influence, given his vested interest in destabilising the current line of succession.

Clarkson is seen as someone who plays the long game, using people as pawns for his own benefit. His ability to cultivate relationships only to discard them when they are no longer useful has earned him a reputation as a social predator.

His desire to extend his influence into the monarchy and government is viewed with suspicion and hostility. Unlike those who serve the crown, Clarkson's motives appear entirely self-serving.

His close ties to Prince Arnold became cemented upon their secret (same sex) marriage, a known disappointment to the royal family, make him a subject of distrust. Many believe he is using Arnold as a means to an end, with no real loyalty to him.

While no formal charges have ever stuck, Clarkson's name has been associated with corruption, bribery, and even threats against political rivals.

Conclusion:

Melvin Clarkson remains a looming threat to the stability of the royal family. His intelligence, wealth, and ability to manipulate powerful figures make him a formidable adversary. If he is indeed connected to the Crown Prince's death, uncovering and exposing his involvement may be the only way to neutralise his influence once and for all.

However, as King Alex himself warned: watch your back. Clarkson is not a man to be taken lightly.

"He sounds like the village idiot to me," Callum commented.

"A very well educated village idiot" warned Blair, it's generally a well educated person that causes trouble and blames it on the village idiot and then acts like the village idiot when the heat gets put on."

"Can we track his movements prior to the avalanche?" Was Mathew's suggestion as he received a cappuccino from the wait staff and ordered the same as yesterday, eggs benedictine. "And, I want to know exactly how the avalanche prevention system works."

Blair silently handed a report to Mathew who suggested that he read it out loud.

"The avalanche avoidance system employed in the region where King Albert III was killed was a state-of-the-art system designed to monitor, predict, and, when necessary, trigger controlled avalanches to prevent catastrophic natural events. Here is a breakdown of the key components of the system." Blair laid the document flat on the dining table and they all shuffled around into a position where they could all read it.

1. Monitoring & Prediction Systems

Seismic Sensors – These were installed in the surrounding mountain regions to detect ground vibrations that could indicate shifting snow masses.

Weather Stations – Real-time data collection on temperature fluctuations, snowfall accumulation, wind patterns, and humidity.

LIDAR & Radar Scanning – Used to detect changes in the snowpack and identify weak layers that might trigger an avalanche.

Drones & Satellite Imaging – Provided updated topographical data and monitored changes in the terrain.

2. Avalanche Control Measures

Explosive Charges (Gazex & Catex Systems) – Gas-powered or cable-mounted explosive devices were strategically placed to trigger controlled avalanches before dangerous levels of snow buildup occurred.

Dynamite Detonations – Occasionally used in more extreme conditions when rapid intervention was required.

Snow Fencing & Barriers – Installed along high-risk slopes to slow down or divert snow movement.

Artificially Triggered Slides – Ski patrol teams and avalanche experts sometimes conducted small controlled slides to prevent larger, unmanageable avalanches.

3. Warning & Evacuation Protocols

Automated Alarm Systems – The area had a network of automated alerts that would notify ski resorts, local authorities, and security teams if avalanche conditions were detected.

Road & Path Closures – Certain mountain roads and ski slopes were subject to immediate closures if the system predicted high-risk conditions.

Rescue & Response Teams – Trained mountain rescue units and ski patrols were always on standby during peak avalanche seasons.

What Went Wrong?

Despite these high-level safety measures, the avalanche that killed King Albert III was unprecedented in its speed and intensity. Investigations initially concluded that:

The avalanche sensors did not trigger the usual warnings, suggesting either a malfunction or interference.

The explosive control measures had not been recently activated, leading to speculation that the snow buildup had reached critical mass unnoticed.

There were irregularities in the maintenance logs, with reports of certain sensors being out of commission for an unexplained period before the disaster.

Weather conditions leading up to the event had been erratic, including sudden warm and cold fluctuations, which might have contributed to the snowpack instability.

Mathew's sharp eye scanned the report, his attention honing in on two critical points: 'Sensor Interference' and 'Unnoticed Snow Buildup.' His instincts immediately flared, these were not mere oversights. They suggested something far more deliberate.

He tapped a finger firmly on the page, emphasising the words as he spoke. "Now, this would indicate to me that human involvement is linked to both of these anomalies," he said, his voice measured but carrying a distinct edge of determination. He lifted his gaze toward Blair, his expression expectant.

"What we need now," he continued, "is the name, or names, of the personnel responsible for these two failures. Someone was in charge of monitoring these systems. Someone either missed something… or made sure it wasn't noticed." His fingers drummed thoughtfully against the paper before he leaned back slightly, waiting for Blair's response.

Blair's eyes narrowed slightly as he processed Mathew's deduction. A slow nod followed, his admiration evident. "Smart… I'm beginning to follow your train of thought, sir." His voice carried a tone of respect, his mind already working through the next steps.

"I have good contacts in that area," he continued, tapping his temple as if to emphasise his network of connections. "If I can get a name, then I can get a background, dig up anything that might explain how this happened, or more importantly, why it happened." A faint smirk played at the corner of his lips. "I'm on it."

With that, Blair turned and strode toward the door, ready to set things in motion. But just as he reached it, he hesitated. A thought struck him, causing him to pivot back toward Mathew.

"Oh, by the way…" His expression darkened slightly. "Callum mentioned that you were about to contact Colonel Pundesh?" He let the question hang for a beat before shaking his head. "I don't trust the man. And I think that in this instance, we should circumvent him."

The weight of his words was unmistakable. Mathew took a slow breath, considering the implications. Clearly, this investigation had just become even more complicated.

Blair had reached out to one of his contacts near St Moritz requesting a full report on the avalanche monitoring station near Corvatsch, the one responsible for the area of the fatal avalanche. Meanwhile he had devised a plan to flush out the leak from the royal house, a simple plan, he contacted Colonel Pundesh and requested travel warrants and and military aircraft to convey HRH Prince Mathew to St Moritz. With allowance for his usual staff to accompany him. He then told Mathew what he had done in the hope that it may get back to the King and that Mathew might give the King the heads up on the 'leak' test.

Later that same day Blair received an email from St Moritz:

Corvatsch Avalanche Monitoring and Control Station

Located in the high alpine region near Piz Corvatsch, the Corvatsch Avalanche Monitoring and Control Station (CAMCS) is a highly specialised facility responsible for overseeing avalanche risk assessment, early warning systems, and mitigation measures across the surrounding slopes and valleys.

Official Mandate:
The station operates under a joint jurisdiction between the Swiss Federal Institute for Snow and Avalanche Research (SLF) and the local Engadin Cantonal Safety Bureau. However, operational control is largely independent, with personnel holding high levels of autonomy due to the unpredictable nature of their work.

Personnel & Chain of Command:

The station is staffed by a small, tightly knit team of seven individuals, all with extensive backgrounds in avalanche control, meteorology, and alpine safety.

Chief of Operations:

Dr. Klaus Meinhardt (53) – A veteran avalanche forecaster with over 25 years of experience in the Swiss Alps. He was trained at

ETH Zurich and worked with the SLF in Davos before being stationed at Corvatsch five years ago. Known for his no-nonsense approach, Meinhardt is deeply respected by his team but has been described as stubborn and resistant to outside interference.

Deputy Chief & Snowpack Specialist:

Marco Rinaldi (41) – An Italian-Swiss avalanche technician with a military background in alpine warfare and rescue. Rinaldi is the station's second-in-command, responsible for monitoring snow stability, conducting field tests, and organising controlled detonations. He has an unofficial reputation for "knowing the mountain" better than anyone. Rinaldi was on duty the night of the King's accident.

Lead Meteorologist:

Dr. Anya Keller (38) – A Swiss climatologist who has worked extensively with weather pattern analysis and atmospheric pressure shifts. Keller is one of the most vocal staff members about potential system failures and had previously raised concerns about sensor interference in the weeks leading up to the avalanche.

Systems & Data Engineer:

Victor Lang (47) – A former private-sector engineer specializing in automated weather stations and seismic sensors. Lang is responsible for ensuring that the station's electronic monitoring system remains operational. His reports indicate that a technical failure or deliberate interference could have occurred the night of the accident.

Field Operations & Rescue Co-ordinator:

Johan Blix (36) – A Swedish avalanche rescue expert, formerly with the International Mountain Rescue Service. Blix is in charge of deploying rescue teams and handling emergency evacuations. He was not on shift the night of the avalanche, as he had taken leave.

Technician & Snow Stability Analyst:

Bruno Eckhart (29) – The youngest member of the team, Eckhart specialises in ground-level snow analysis, including measuring snow depth, density, and movement. He is an absolute legend when it comes to repairing or modifying the sensitive instruments or anything electronic. His logs on un-noticed snow buildup were incomplete, and his absence on key nights has raised some speculation about his reliability.

Station Administrator & Liaison:

Marta Von Hohenfels (30) – The station's administrative officer, in charge of handling official reports, co-ordinating with Cantonal Authorities, and maintaining operational records. Von Hohenfels is the newest and only non-technical member of the team, though her knowledge of past incidents makes her an important witness.

Suspicious Elements in the Avalanche Investigation

Sensor Interference: Victor Lang and Dr. Keller both noted unexplained fluctuations in telemetry data two days before the avalanche. Bruno Eckhart had reported a battery failure with some equipment and he had replaced the faulty batteries with new. This was attributed to the instrument fluctuations.

Un-noticed Snow Buildup: Bruno Eckhart's incomplete records suggest that certain areas of the mountain may not have been properly monitored in the 48 hours leading up to the incident.

Bruno explained his records were lagging because of spending time replacing batteries.

Personnel Movements: Marco Rinaldi was on duty the night of the avalanche, meaning he had direct control over detonation schedules and safety measures. He was absent for a brief period due to a gastric complaint.

Access to External Parties: The station has been visited twice in the last year by Melvin Clarkson and his corporate representatives, allegedly to evaluate investment opportunities in winter tourism technology and to ensure the winter guests safety.

A note at the end of the report indicated that it was the same document that had been provided to MI5 and MI6. Both agencies had reviewed the report without raising any questions. Mathew placed the report on his desk, disbelief etched across his face as he stared at Blair. "Fucking Clarkson… and no one asked any fucking questions… you've got to be joking!" Mathew could hardly wrap his mind around it. "And where do these reports go once they leave MI5 and MI6?"

Blair answered calmly, "Hugh Drinkwater receives it for his ratification. After that, MI5 and MI6 await further instructions once they've forwarded the report. This particular one is produced by sources from Interpol. We can only assume the Swiss authorities have access to it for their own actions."

Mathew leaned back in his chair, processing the information. "So, if Hugh Drinkwater is satisfied that everything in this report is above board, it doesn't go any further?" He was beginning to piece together the system. "Drinkwater would know who Clarkson is... I presume?"

Blair thought for a moment before replying, "One would think so… but perhaps not. Clarkson had been banned from all royal premises by the Queen, after all. Maybe 'Drinkie' doesn't know who he is." He paused, considering the possibility. "But, frankly, I think that's highly unlikely."

Mathew shook his head in frustration. "This whole thing is a bloody mess." He rubbed his temples, trying to make sense of the tangled web. Blair's assessment didn't help ease the weight of the situation, but it was a piece of the puzzle, nonetheless.

Max Barrington

After careful consideration, Mathew turned to Blair. "I need you to contact every tavern, bar, and pub in and around St. Moritz. Give them a photo of Clarkson, along with a generous incentive, and ask them to review their security footage. If they find any footage of Clarkson drinking in their establishment, have them send it to you immediately." His tone was firm, leaving no room for misinterpretation.

Blair nodded sharply. "Onto it, sir!" Without wasting another second, he clicked into action, disappearing from the room to set the plan in motion.

Just as Blair left, a page entered the room, bowing slightly before delivering his message. "Your Royal Highness, the King requests your presence in his office at three o'clock this afternoon."

Mathew exhaled slowly, running a hand through his hair. He had been expecting this summons, he just wasn't sure if it was about Clarkson, the report, or something else entirely. Either way, he had little choice but to comply. He dismissed the page with a nod and turned back to his desk, glancing once more at the damning report before him. Whatever the King had to say, Mathew knew one thing for certain, this day was far from over.

The King certainly didn't look pleased. His expression was hard, his lips pressed into a thin line, but Mathew didn't know him well enough yet to judge whether this was frustration, anger, or merely his natural demeanour.

"I think it would have been respectful, if not prudent, to inform me that you were off gallivanting to Switzerland," the King said coldly, his eyes locked onto Mathew with a steely gaze as he awaited an explanation.

Mathew forced himself to remain composed, though his pulse quickened. He had to be careful, very careful. Keeping his voice level, he replied, "I'm not going anywhere, sir. May I ask where you heard that I was traveling to Switzerland?" He chose his words deliberately, hoping he wasn't overstepping.

The King's face darkened further, his skin flushing red with barely contained fury. Then, in a voice that boomed through the room like a thunderclap, he erupted.

"From fucking ARNOLD!… OF.. ALL… fucking people!

YOU….NEED to tell ME what you are DOING! Do you understand me, BOY?"

Mathew held his ground, though the force of the King's outburst made his ears ring. It took several tense minutes of careful explanations before he was finally able to get the King to calm down.

"Sir," Mathew began carefully, "Blair Washington requested travel warrants for myself and my immediate staff to St. Moritz. No one else was informed of this request, except me. And now, you're telling me that Arnold somehow has full knowledge of my fake travel plans?" He let that hang in the air for a moment before continuing. "I ask you, sir, doesn't that strike you as a little strange?"

The King's nostrils flared as he processed the information. Mathew could see the shift in his expression, his anger hadn't dissipated, but now it was mingled with something else. Realisation. Doubt.

A heavy silence settled over the room as the King mulled over what Mathew had just laid before him. Slowly, the tension in his face eased, and the deep red flush faded, returning his complexion to its usual buff tone. A slight grin curled the corners of his lips, and when he finally spoke, his voice had lost its previous fury, replaced instead with something far more measured, almost amused.

"Have you found the leak, Mathew?" His grin widened into a warm, mischievous smile as he leaned forward slightly. "Who is it, Mathew?… Who is it?"

Mathew allowed himself to breathe a little easier, though he remained cautious. He had the answer, or at least a very strong suspicion, but this wasn't entirely his victory to claim.

"Blair Washington would be the best to consult in this instance, sir," Mathew replied smoothly. "It was he who placed the travel warrant request, and to whom it was submitted, I have my suspicions, but I cannot say with absolute certainty just yet."

In truth, Mathew was quite sure that Colonel Pundesh was the source of the leak. It had been Blair who had filed the request, and if the information had made its way to Arnold, then Pundesh was the most likely link in the chain. But Mathew saw no need to take the credit for himself. This had been Blair's plan, and if anyone deserved the moment of revelation, it was him.

The King studied Mathew for a long moment before nodding approvingly. "Very well. Have Washington report to me as soon as he has something concrete."

Mathew inclined his head. "Yes, sir."

The King leaned back in his chair, still smiling to himself, the flicker of intrigue now evident in his eyes. "This should be interesting." The King was warming considerably to Mathew. His previous frustration had melted away, replaced by something almost akin to camaraderie.

"Oh, and by the way," he said casually, "I understand there have been snooker games in the bar lounge every night as of late. I should very much like to be invited this evening." He paused briefly, then added with a grin, "In fact, I think I'll stay for dinner as well."

Turning his attention to the aide standing attentively by the wall, he gave a quick nod. "Get that organised, will you? The chef knows what to put on the menu for me." With that, he looked back at Mathew, his tone light but expectant. "I'll see you at dinner, Mathew."

And just like that, the meeting was over. Mathew inclined his head in acknowledgment before being excused.

Once outside the King's office, he immediately sought out Callum. "I need you to contact Blair and tell him to report to the King regarding the discovery of the leak's source," he instructed.

Callum gave a sharp nod. "Right away."

"One more thing," Mathew added. "The King will be joining the three of us for dinner and snooker this evening. Make sure Blair gets the 'heads up', I'd rather he not be blindsided."

A knowing smirk crossed Callum's face. "Understood."

As Callum set off to relay the message, Mathew allowed himself a small smile. The King's interest in their snooker games was unexpected, but perhaps this was his way of testing the waters, of building rapport. Whatever the reason, one thing was certain: tonight's game was shaping up to be far more than just a casual round of snooker.

At precisely six-thirty that evening, Mathew, accompanied by Callum, who maintained the precise, regulated two steps behind and slightly to the right, entered the bar for pre-dinner drinks. The atmosphere was warm and relaxed, the low hum of conversation mingling with the clink of glasses.

Already seated and engaged in easy conversation were the King and his equerry, David Patterson. Across from them, Blair Washington sat with a tumbler in hand, looking particularly at ease. It was clear from the way they spoke that Blair had already been drawn into the fold.

Mathew and Callum joined them, ordering their drinks just as the butler arrived to announce that dinner was served. The five men made their way to the dining room, where the table had been set for an informal yet elegant meal. Conversation remained light and pleasant as they moved through the first course, touching on sports, travel, and the latest gossip circulating within the palace.

But as the meal progressed, the discussion inevitably turned to more serious matters. When the topic of the security leak arose, the King leaned forward slightly, his expression sharpening with interest.

"So," he said, swirling his wine glass thoughtfully, "you nailed that bastard Pundesh, Blair. Well done. I must commend you on the brilliance of the plan." He paused, setting down his glass as his gaze fixed on Blair. "Do you believe he acted alone? Or do you suspect he was passing information to others?"

The shift in the room was subtle but unmistakable. The easy camaraderie from earlier gave way to something more focused, more deliberate. All eyes turned to Blair, waiting for his assessment.

Blair took a measured sip of his drink before setting the glass down with deliberate care. His expression remained composed, but there was a quiet satisfaction in his tone as he answered the King's question.

"MI5 is certain that the leaked information was confined to His Majesty Prince Arnold," he began. "However, there is a strong possibility that it was then passed on to Melvin Clarkson. And from there…" he exhaled lightly, shaking his head. "Well, from there, it could have gone anywhere."

The King's jaw tightened slightly at the mention of Melvin's name, but he said nothing, merely gesturing for Blair to continue.

"Well, everything being said," Blair added with quiet finality, "there will, or should, be no further passing of classified information." His voice carried an unmistakable weight, a certainty that left little room for doubt.

A beat of silence followed, the implication hanging heavy over the table. It was clear, whoever had been responsible for the leaks had been shut down, and the breach had been sealed. The only question that remained was what the King intended to do about it.

A game of snooker played by double's with Blair and Callum, versus the King and the Prince. A total of three games resulted in the King and the Prince winning two games to one. David Paterson, the King's equerry became the referee for the three games and not without some jovial arguments.

Following the games there was a last drinks and cigar's in the lounge, the King did ask if there was any news on the avalanche internal investigation. Mathew got in very quick to answer that

                                    Max Barrington

there may be some information later this week, but nothing as yet. He glanced at Callum and Blair as if to say, "no more information" and the subject was closed and the evening came to an end.

On page three of The London Times, nestled among the day's lesser headlines, a small but noteworthy article reported on a fatal single-vehicle accident that had occurred on the Westway freeway near Notting Hill.

According to the report, the incident involved a black Range Rover that had inexplicably veered off the road, slamming into a concrete pylon with devastating force. Emergency services arrived swiftly, but there was little they could do, Lt. Col. Roger Pundesh, the sole occupant of the vehicle, had been killed instantly upon impact.

The article offered no speculation on the cause of the accident, merely noting that authorities were investigating the circumstances surrounding the crash. However, for those who knew the name Pundesh, the implications were far more significant than the brief column space suggested.

On his scheduled day off, the duty manager of the Hotel Steffani, located on Via Somplaz, took it upon himself to personally review the surveillance footage from the hotel's lounge bar. The request for information had been accompanied by a generous retainer, making it well worth his time. Carefully sifting through the specified dates, he meticulously examined the recordings, fast-forwarding through hours of footage with a practiced eye.

His efforts were soon rewarded. There, captured in crisp clarity, was the very individual shown in the photograph that had accompanied the inquiry. The match was undeniable.

Satisfied with his findings, the manager wasted no time. He reached for his phone and made contact with the person who had submitted the request, ready to deliver the crucial piece of evidence they had been searching for.

The hotel manager was duly rewarded as promised, the generous compensation making his efforts more than worthwhile. However, his contact offered an additional incentive, an even greater reward if he could successfully identify the individuals with whom the subject had interacted during his time in the lounge bar. The prospect of further financial gain sharpened his focus, and he eagerly set about reviewing the footage once more, determined to extract every possible detail.

Meanwhile, a copy of the surveillance recording was discreetly forwarded, under the strictest confidence, to Dr. Klaus Meinhardt, the head of operations at the Corvatsch Monitoring and Prediction Centre. The footage arrived with an urgent request for review, and upon examining it, Dr. Meinhardt's expression darkened.

He immediately recognised one of the men in the video, Melvin Clarkson. The name alone was cause for concern. Clarkson had previously approached the centre under the pretence of seeking knowledge about their advanced avalanche warning systems, claiming he needed the information to reassure guests at ski lodges and resorts. At the time, his inquiry had raised few alarms. Now, however, his presence in this context painted a far more troubling picture.

But what truly unsettled Dr. Meinhardt was the second figure beside Clarkson in the footage. It was none other than Bruno Eckhart, a former employee of the centre, one who had left under less than amicable circumstances. The sight of Eckhart in Clarkson's company on the evening in question suggested that their meeting was no mere coincidence.

Dr. Meinhardt leaned back in his chair, exhaling sharply. This new revelation posed far more questions than answers, and none of them were comforting. He passed this information to Blair Washington.

The hotel duty manager had been diligently showing the surveillance footage to a wide circle of acquaintances, each time hoping to secure a definitive identification of the individuals seen in the company of Melvin Clarkson that evening. His persistence finally paid off when one contact, after studying the recording carefully, hesitated for a moment before speaking.

"I'm about eighty percent certain," the man said cautiously, "that the third person sitting at the table with Clarkson is Aldrich Müller."

The name carried weight. Müller was known in certain circles as a small-time criminal and a standover merchant, someone who operated in the shadows, exerting pressure on those who owed debts or had something to hide. Wasting no time, the duty manager quickly relayed this information to Blair Washington, eager to secure the additional reward he had been promised. He assured Washington that he remained fully committed to assisting further in any way he could.

Forwarding Müllers name to MI5 had produced further information.

Aldrich Müller – Background Dossier:

Name: Aldrich Müller
Aliases: "Al," "The Fixer"
Nationality: Swiss-German
Age: Mid-50s
Known Affiliations: Various underworld figures across Switzerland, Germany, and Austria
Criminal Activities: Extortion, intimidation, black-market dealings, discreet 'problem resolution' services

Aldrich Müller has long operated in the grey spaces between legitimate business and organised crime, earning a reputation as a small-time criminal with powerful connections. While never linked to any single organisation, he is known to have worked with elements of the Swiss underworld, particularly in Zurich and Geneva, as well as in Austria and southern Germany. His primary expertise lies in intimidation and coercion, often posing as a "consultant" to resolve financial or personal disputes, usually in a manner that favours his employer.

Criminal Profile & Methods:

Müller built his career on being a standover merchant, using a mix of charm and menace to enforce debts, silence inconvenient individuals, or ensure cooperation in delicate matters. He operates with a level of sophistication that sets him apart from common street enforcers. He rarely uses direct violence himself, instead relying on psychological pressure, blackmail, and well-placed threats to get results.

Ties to the Financial Underground:
Müller has been linked to discreet financial dealings involving money laundering, offshore accounts, and fraudulent investments. He has reportedly facilitated the movement of illicit funds through Swiss banks, though authorities have never been able to tie him directly to such operations.

Political and Corporate Espionage
There have been whispers that Müller has, on occasion, acted as an information broker, selling sensitive data to interested parties. He has been seen in the company of mid-level political figures and corporate executives, suggesting a more complex role beyond simple thuggery.

Previous Investigations:
Despite numerous suspicions and occasional arrests, Müller has never been convicted of a serious crime. He is known for his meticulous approach, ensuring that any operation he is involved in leaves little to no direct evidence tying him to wrongdoing. Law enforcement agencies in Switzerland and Germany consider him a person of interest, but his ability to stay just within the bounds of legality has kept him free.

Connection to Melvin Clarkson:

Müller's presence at the St. Moritz hotel bar alongside Melvin Clarkson and Bruno Eckhart raises significant concerns. Clarkson, already a suspect in relation to the avalanche investigation, has no known prior connections to Müller, at least, none that are officially documented. If Müller was involved in whatever Clarkson and

Eckhart were discussing, it suggests the operation may extend beyond a simple breach of confidential information.

Given Müller's history with financial schemes and coercion, it is possible that his role in this meeting was to facilitate an exchange, either of information, money, or influence. Alternatively, he may have been acting as an intermediary between Clarkson and a yet-unknown third party.

Current Whereabouts & Risk Assessment

Aldrich Müller is believed to divide his time between Zurich, Geneva, and Vienna, though he is known to frequent high-end ski resorts, casinos, and exclusive private clubs across Europe. His ability to blend seamlessly into high society while maintaining ties to the criminal underworld makes him an elusive and potentially dangerous figure.

Given his presence with Clarkson, it is imperative to establish whether he is merely an associate or an active participant in whatever scheme is unfolding. His involvement suggests a level of complexity beyond what was initially suspected.

On a sudden whim, Blair asked MI5 to check if the Corvatsch Monitoring and Prediction Centre had any surveillance equipment and if it did to view the footage from at least two weeks prior to the avalanche and to take extracts of any footage showing Clarkson, Müller and Eckhart. He also asked for a full dossier on Bruno Eckhart.

Mathew was eager to dedicate every moment of his time to working alongside Blair in what was rapidly unfolding into a thrilling and intricate pursuit. The investigation had taken on an urgency and complexity that excited him, and he was determined to see it through. However, his newfound position within the royal family of Wynasleigh came with its own set of expectations, expectations that required him to take a more structured and co-operative approach to understanding both the intricacies of the monarchy and its historical and functional ties to the nation.

A significant part of this education revolved around the family's deep-rooted connection to the Church, an institution that had been interwoven with the monarchy for centuries. This was not merely a symbolic relationship but one that carried real influence, governance, and responsibilities. Mathew was expected to invest considerable time and effort in studying these ties, which meant long hours of historical and theological discussions, often in the company of both the Supreme Governor of the Church and the Archbishop.

While the thrill of the chase with Blair beckoned him, Mathew knew that he could not neglect this other aspect of his new life. He would need to strike a careful balance, immersing himself in the traditions and obligations of the royal house while still keeping one foot firmly in the world of intelligence and investigation. How well he managed this delicate duality would ultimately define his role within both realms.

A grand Royal Banquet was set to take place the following week at the Palace in honour of **HRH Prince Mathew**. The event was to be an elegant and exclusive gathering, with no less than one hundred and fifty guests invited, marking a significant occasion in Mathew's new life within the royal fold. The guest list was an impressive one, with dignitaries, ambassadors, and nobility from across Europe, but at the very top of the list was **HRH Prince Arnold**, the monarch's son. It seemed that Mathew was finally going to meet the elusive Arnold, a figure who had been a subject of curiosity and intrigue since his arrival.

However, what caught Mathew's attention was the conspicuous absence of Arnold's spouse, Melvin Clarkson, from the guest list. It was an interesting omission, considering Clarkson's usual proximity to the Prince. Mathew couldn't help but wonder if there was some sort of subtle political manoeuvre at play.

Callum, ever the pragmatist, quickly put Mathew's mind at ease. "The name on the invitation is more for the sake of appearances, sir," Callum explained. "Arnold won't be attending alone. He would never show up without Clarkson. But rest assured, Clarkson hasn't been invited." The reassurance helped alleviate some of Mathew's unease. The prospect of not meeting Arnold and Clarkson seemed far more manageable.

For a moment, Mathew felt a sense of relief, he could face the event without the looming presence of Arnold complicating matters. Yet, just as Mathew allowed himself to relax, Callum dropped the last bit of information with an almost casual air, "But, I suppose they may both attend, just the same?"

The casual mention of Arnolds's potential attendance stirred a subtle anxiety in Mathew. It was as though, despite all assurances, there was still some unpredictable element in play, something out of his control. Why would Clarkson not be invited, but the possibility of his appearance still lingered? Mathew couldn't shake the nagging feeling that this would be far from a straightforward gathering.

In preparation for the upcoming Royal Banquet, Mathew's presence was required at the Palace for an important session with the Lord Steward, who was tasked with educating him on the intricacies of the event. This meeting was not merely a formality, it was a deep dive into the etiquette, customs, and protocol that governed the royal functions. Mathew was to learn the fine details of banquet procedures, from the proper order of seating to the unspoken rules that dictated every action, gesture, and conversation in the room. It was a world steeped in tradition, where every movement was deliberate, and every word measured. Mathew's role was to not only participate but to do so with the grace and understanding expected of someone in his position.

After his session with the Lord Steward, Mathew was given a tour of the Palace by the Lord Chamberlain. As they moved through the grand halls and intimate spaces, the Lord Chamberlain explained the history and significance of each area, highlighting the traditions that had been upheld for centuries. Mathew found himself captivated by the timeless elegance of the Palace, each room filled with echoes of history, its walls adorned with portraits and tapestries of royal ancestors. It was clear that every corner of the Palace had its own story to tell.

The tour concluded with an informal meeting with the King and Queen, an opportunity for Mathew to interact with the sovereigns in a more relaxed, personal setting. This meeting, while informal, was nonetheless crucial. The King and Queen's presence was an indication of their interest in Mathew's integration into the royal family, and their warmth helped ease some of the tension he had felt earlier. The conversation was light but insightful, with the royal couple asking about Mathew's experiences and his thoughts on the upcoming event. They shared a few anecdotes, offering glimpses into the royal lifestyle, making Mathew feel more at ease in their company.

Despite the casual tone of the meeting, Mathew knew that these interactions were part of a larger process of assimilation, a way for him to understand the delicate balance between formality and

                    Max Barrington

familiarity within the royal household. It was clear that he was being groomed not just as a guest at the banquet, but as a member of the royal circle, someone whose actions and presence would be scrutinised. As the meeting concluded, the Queen asked Mathew if he had any updates on the avalanche investigation, Mathew answered with a "Not yet ma'am , you will be the first to know I can assure you."

The Banquet

Mathew stood at the entrance of the grand hall, precisely where he had been instructed to be. He was positioned on the far left side, next to the King and the Queen, ready to greet the distinguished guests arriving for the Royal Banquet. His posture was impeccable, a reflection of all the guidance and rehearsals he had undergone in the days leading up to this event. As each guest arrived, Mathew dutifully stood by the King and Queen, listening carefully to the Royal Usher as they announced the names of the dignitaries making their entrance.

With each introduction, Mathew's nerves gradually faded, replaced by a growing sense of confidence. This was what he had trained for, the royal protocols, the formalities, and the precise order in which everything was to unfold. He smiled warmly as each guest was introduced to their Royal Highnesses, exchanging pleasantries and making small talk, ensuring that his demeanour was polished and respectful. It was a world of refined gestures and carefully chosen words, and Mathew had become well accustomed to it.

However, when the fifth introduction came, it took Mathew completely by surprise. As the Royal Usher called out the names of the next arrivals, Mathew's gaze instinctively lifted, and there, walking towards him with undeniable poise, was His Royal Highness Prince Arnold, the King's son, flanked by none other than Melvin Clarkson.

The Queen had excused herself and sought The Lord Steward who was already making adjustment to the dining places. Clarkson may not have been invited but he certainly was not going to embarrass the royal family at their banquet.

The very sight of Clarkson stirred something deep within Mathew, a mixture of disbelief and unease. He had been assured that Clarkson had not been invited, yet here he was, standing at the threshold of the banquet in the company of the Prince. This was

Max Barrington

no coincidence. Clarkson's presence was a stark reminder that even in royal circles, nothing was ever quite as simple as it seemed.

The Royal Usher smoothly made the introduction, and Mathew, though taken aback, maintained his composure. "Your Royal Highness, it's an honour to meet you," Mathew said with a slight bow to Prince Arnold, his voice steady, though his thoughts raced. He then turned to Clarkson, offering him a polite nod, his smile strained as he greeted the man who had been both an enigma and a source of tension since Mathew's arrival. "Mr. Clarkson, a pleasure," Mathew added, trying to mask the underlying discomfort in his voice.

The exchange was brief, and the conversation that followed felt strained, as if both Mathew and Clarkson were measuring each other with every word. Clarkson, for his part, was the epitome of controlled indifference, his expression unreadable as he offered a slight nod in return. Prince Arnold, on the other hand, seemed to be enjoying the moment, his demeanour as charming as ever, though Mathew couldn't shake the feeling that there was more to this meeting than met the eye.

As they moved further into the hall, Mathew couldn't help but wonder what the real purpose of Clarkson's presence was, whether it was a subtle power play or if something more sinister was afoot. One thing was clear: the evening, which had already held its share of surprises, had just become far more complex.

The Royal Banquet was an event of extraordinary elegance and opulence, a grand affair that dazzled with its meticulous attention to detail. The venue, the magnificent Palace Hall, had been transformed into a lavish dining space, with its high ceilings and chandeliers casting a soft, golden glow over the gathering. Tables were arranged in a grand semi-circle, each draped in rich, royal blue fabric, adorned with sparkling crystal goblets, polished silverware, and intricately folded napkins. The room was filled with the faint scent of fresh flowers, their vibrant colours adding to the warmth of the evening.

The banquet was attended by an array of guests from various backgrounds, noblemen and women, diplomats, esteemed dignitaries, and family members of the royal household, all dressed in their finest attire. The atmosphere was charged with a sense of formality, yet there was a palpable undercurrent of excitement, as this was an evening not only of celebration but also of forging connections and strengthening bonds within the royal circles.

As the guests settled into their seats, the King and Queen took their places at the head of the table, with Mathew and other key members of the royal family beside them. The Royal Usher discreetly signalled the start of the evening, and the first course was served.

Appetisers were a sophisticated array of delicacies. A platter of smoked salmon canapés rested before each guest, topped with a delicate cream cheese mousse and garnished with a sliver of lemon zest. Alongside this, there were miniature pâtés en croûte, rich with flavours of foie gras and truffle, offering an indulgent start to the evening's culinary delights. The light, crisp vegetable terrine with a honeyed glaze was served next, paired with a refreshing citrus vinaigrette that balanced the richness of the other appetisers.

The main course was a masterful presentation of both elegance and grandeur. Roast lamb was the highlight, its tender, perfectly seared meat served with a rosemary and red wine reduction, the savoury aroma filling the room as it was presented to each guest. Accompanying the lamb was a medley of perfectly roasted vegetables, baby carrots, wild mushrooms, and parsnips, each seasoned to perfection and roasted until golden. The potato dauphinoise, thinly sliced potatoes baked in cream, garlic, and Gruyère cheese, was a rich and indulgent side dish that complemented the meat beautifully. For those who preferred a lighter option, a perfectly prepared grilled sea bass was offered, served with a light, herb-infused beurre blanc sauce and a delicate lemon wedge.

                    Max Barrington

As the courses continued, guests were treated to a cheese course, a selection of the finest cheeses, Brie de Meaux, Comté, and a pungent Roquefort, served with an assortment of freshly baked breads and fig compote, adding a sweet contrast to the richness of the cheeses.

The dessert course was a true masterpiece. A stunning trio of petit fours arrived at the table, each more decadent than the last. There was a silky dark chocolate mousse in delicate gold-edged cups, a raspberry sorbet that provided a refreshing contrast to the richness of the meal, and a luxurious tiramisu with layers of mascarpone cream and a dusting of cocoa. Each dessert was a harmonious blend of textures and flavours, designed to delight the senses.

To conclude the meal, a selection of fine wines, a crisp Chablis, a robust Bordeaux, and a sweet Sauternes, was paired with each course, and guests sipped their drinks in conversation, allowing the flavours of the evening to settle.

Throughout the banquet, the conversation flowed smoothly, though Mathew couldn't help but feel a sense of unease whenever Prince Arnold and Melvin Clarkson engaged in dialogue nearby. The usual pleasantries were exchanged, but Mathew couldn't shake the feeling that something far more complicated was unfolding beneath the surface. Despite his unease, he knew the evening was about more than just food and drink; it was about establishing relationships, making alliances, and ensuring his place within the royal fold.

After the lavish dinner, the guests retreated to the grand drawing room to enjoy the finer pleasures of the evening, ports of exceptional quality and carefully selected cigars, their rich, smoky aroma filling the air. The gentlemen, their conversation now more relaxed and informal, gathered around deep, plush armchairs and a few ornate side tables adorned with decanters and crystal glasses. Meanwhile, the ladies had their own space, sipping tea and enjoying lighter cocktails, like gin and tonics, in the adjoining sitting room. The atmosphere in the drawing room was one of refinement, yet it was clear that many of the men were more inclined to let down their guard after the formality of the banquet.

It was during this transition that Melvin Clarkson, ever the enigmatic and unpredictable figure, moved toward Mathew with a confident, almost predatory air. His approach was subtle, his movements deliberate, and as he reached Mathew, he paused, his gaze briefly flickering over the room before turning his attention fully to him.

"Your Highness," Clarkson began, his voice smooth but carrying an edge that hinted at something more, "Could I trouble you for a moment of your time?" Without waiting for Mathew's consent, he pressed on, his tone flat but menacing, "Roger Pundesh was my friend!…Tell Blair Washington... he's fucked."

With that, Clarkson offered a final glance, one that lingered long enough for Mathew to read the quiet threat behind it. Without another word, Clarkson turned on his heel and walked away, leaving Mathew standing in the thickening haze of cigar smoke, the tension from his abrupt message hanging heavy in the air.

The room seemed to grow quieter, as if the weight of Clarkson's words had cast a shadow over the evening's lively atmosphere. Mathew, somewhat taken aback by the cold directness of the message, was left standing, processing what had just transpired. He knew that Clarkson's words were no mere passing comment; they were a declaration, an open challenge.

A wave of unease swept over Mathew as he considered how best to handle this unexpected communication. What had happened to bring about such hostility? And more importantly, why had Clarkson chosen him as the messenger?

The evening had taken a distinct turn, and Mathew knew that whatever followed would have profound consequences for Blair Washington and, likely, for the royal family. Clarkson's words were a warning, and Mathew understood that in the dangerous game of politics and intrigue that swirled around the royal circles, no one was immune from the fallout.

Mathew turned sharply toward Callum, who stood dutifully just three meters away. Callum had been watching Clarkson's approach closely, his instincts already on high alert. As soon as Clarkson abruptly turned and walked away, Callum had started moving toward Mathew, only to hesitate when it became clear that no immediate confrontation had occurred. Now, seeing the urgency in Mathew's expression, Callum relaxed slightly, until Mathew gave him a subtle nod, signalling him closer.

"Sir?" Callum asked, his voice low but attentive, his eyes flicking briefly in the direction where Clarkson had vanished.

Mathew leaned in, speaking just above a whisper. "We must get a message to Blair, I think he may be in danger. Quickly, go and tell him to be careful." His concern was unmistakable, his voice edged with urgency. He then repeated Clarkson's words verbatim, the weight of the threat settling between them.

Callum's jaw tightened. "I can't leave you," he said, his tone firm but measured. "We could both go, but I doubt that would be advisable. I'll try to reach him discreetly on my mobile. Let's move somewhere with fewer eyes."

With practiced ease, Callum guided Mathew toward a quieter corner of the room, away from the thickening clusters of gentlemen engaged in post-dinner conversation. There, shielded by the ambient hum of voices and the haze of cigar smoke, Callum pulled out his phone and dialled Blair's number.

The call rang. Once. Twice. Three times. No answer. Callum's frown deepened as he lowered the phone, shaking his head. "He's not picking up."

Mathew's stomach tightened. "Try again."

Callum redialed. Still nothing. He exhaled slowly. "There could be countless reasons why he's not answering," he said, though his voice lacked conviction.

Mathew's mind raced. "We can't just sit here. Call Drinkwater. Get him to check on Blair."

Max Barrington

With nothing to lose, Callum swiftly dialled Hugh Drinkwater, the external head of security. When the call connected, Callum spoke with crisp precision, relaying Clarkson's exact words to Mathew and the underlying sense of menace they carried.

"We need you to make contact with Blair immediately," Callum said, his voice firm but quiet.

Drinkwater, a man of few words, didn't hesitate. "Understood. I'll get back to you as soon as I have something."

Meanwhile, Mathew resumed his role, continuing to meet and exchange pleasantries with various dignitaries, ever aware of Callum standing just behind his right shoulder, silent, watchful, and ever dutiful. The evening was drawing to a close, the grandeur of the royal banquet giving way to murmured farewells as guests began to take their leave. It was nearing six o'clock when Callum's phone vibrated discreetly in his pocket. He answered it with a curt, professional efficiency, his expression darkening slightly as he listened.

Mathew, still engaged in conversation, noticed the subtle change in Callum's demeanour. When the call ended, Callum leaned in ever so slightly and spoke in a quiet, controlled tone.

"Blair Washington, it seems, is missing," he said, his voice barely above a whisper.

Mathew felt an immediate jolt of unease, though his expression remained composed.

"Drinkie will meet us in his office in ten minutes," Callum continued, referring to Hugh Drinkwater, the head of external security. He cast a quick glance around the room, noting the steadily dwindling number of guests.

Then, with a subtle nod toward a side exit, he murmured, "Follow me, sir."

Mathew needed no further prompting. Without hesitation, he fell into step behind Callum, leaving behind the fading echoes of laughter and polite conversation as they made their way toward what now felt like some bad business of the evening.

"Apparently, Blair received a call in his office earlier this evening, informing him that he needed to contact home urgently, his dog had reportedly been hit by a car," Hugh Drinkwater explained, his voice measured but laced with concern.

"His secretary said he immediately tried calling his home number, but there was no answer. He then attempted to reach his wife's mobile, but it went straight to voicemail. Unable to get through, he decided to drive home himself, and that, gentlemen, is the last anyone has heard from him."

Drinkwater reached into his folder and retrieved a single sheet of paper, handing it to Callum.

"It's all here for your record, Callum."

Then, turning to Mathew, his expression grew more serious.

"We've already got patrol units canvassing the area, searching for his car. We've also spoken with his wife, she claims she hasn't heard a word from him all evening." He paused, allowing the weight of that statement to settle before adding, "And as for their dog, the supposed reason for the emergency? They have two, actually... and both are perfectly fine."

The room was silent for a moment as the weight of the revelation settled over them like a heavy fog. Mathew felt a knot tighten in his stomach, a sinking certainty gripping him. He exhaled sharply, his voice low but resolute.

"This was a setup. Blair was lured out, and now he's vanished!"

Hugh Drinkwater, arms crossed, let out a measured breath before responding, his tone careful.

"With all due respect, sir, I think you're jumping to rather... dramatic conclusions."

Mathew's gaze darkened, his jaw tightening as he took a step closer.

"Am I?" He met Drinkwater's eyes, his voice now edged with urgency. "Because this afternoon, at the banquet, Melvin Clarkson sidled up to me, uninvited, and left me with a message to pass on to Blair."

Drinkwater's expression remained neutral, though a flicker of interest crossed his face.

"And what, exactly, did he say?"

Mathew didn't blink. "He said,...Roger Pundesh was my friend!..Tell him... he's fucked."

The colour drained from Drinkwater's face. His lips parted slightly, as if to speak, but no words came. His throat worked as he swallowed, his stance shifting. The composed exterior cracked just enough for Mathew to see that he was no longer the only one feeling that knot in his gut.

The pieces were falling into place, and the picture they painted was far from reassuring.

Drinkwater barely finished his sentence before realising the absurdity of his own question. He shook his head, correcting himself swiftly.

"Forget I asked, sir. That was a foolish question." His expression hardened with renewed focus. "I'd best get the Chief Superintendent from The Yard involved immediately."

Before he could move, the shrill ring of his mobile phone cut through the tense atmosphere. He answered it with clipped efficiency, listening intently for only a few moments before his face set into a grim mask. With a slow, deliberate motion, he ended the call and exhaled sharply.

"The Chief Superintendent is already on his way." His voice was measured, but there was an unmistakable weight to it. He met Mathew's gaze with something akin to reluctant resignation. "They've just found Blair Washington's body, it was in his car with a single gunshot wound to his head."

     Max Barrington

Silence stretched between them for a beat, the finality of those words sinking in.

"I need to beg your indulgence, sir," Drinkwater continued, his tone quieter but no less resolute. "I'd ask that you wait here to speak with the Chief Superintendent when he arrives."

Callum exhaled sharply and pulled out his phone. "I'd better let the boss know," he muttered, dialling the King's personal secretary.

The call took longer than expected. Callum spoke in hushed, measured tones, his expression unreadable. When he finally ended the call, he turned to Mathew, his face grim.

"It's on you, sir." His voice was steady, but there was an unmistakable weight behind his words. "You're to handle this personally and keep His Majesty informed."

He held Mathew's gaze for a moment, then added, more softly, "I don't need to tell you what that means."

"I guess I'm in charge of this situation" Mathew said soberly.

Chief Superintendent Neville Fleming of the London Metropolitan Police arrived promptly at Hugh Drinkwater's office, accompanied by Inspector Dennis Proud. Both men carried the air of seasoned officers, calm, efficient, and quietly assessing everything around them.

As introductions were made, Fleming's posture stiffened slightly upon meeting His Royal Highness Prince Mathew. With a respectful nod, he wasted no time in addressing the formality of the situation.

"Your Highness, if you prefer, I can have the Chief Constable oversee this matter personally," Fleming offered, his tone measured but deferential.

Mathew met his gaze evenly. "That won't be necessary, Chief Superintendent. I have every confidence that you are more than capable of handling this investigation."

Fleming inclined his head in appreciation, then took out his notepad as Mathew briefed him on the events leading up to Blair Washington's disappearance. He recounted the urgent phone call that lured Blair from his office, his subsequent vanishing, and the chilling message delivered by Melvin Clarkson earlier that evening.

As Mathew spoke, Inspector Proud took notes, his brow furrowing deeper with every detail. When Mathew finished, a heavy silence settled in the room.

Chief Superintendent Neville Fleming straightened his posture, his expression cooling as he regarded Mathew with a measured gaze. "Well, Your Highness, it would appear that Mr. Clarkson, in this instance, has an alibi. He was seen leaving the palace shortly after the conclusion of the banquet." His tone was crisp, professional, and unmistakably firm.

Mathew's brows furrowed in disbelief. "You've already checked and confirmed the times, Chief Superintendent?" His voice carried a hint of skepticism. "Impossible! You've only just arrived."

The room fell into a tense silence.

Fleming's eyes darkened slightly, his jaw tightening. The subtle shift in his demeanour did not go unnoticed. Mathew realised, perhaps a second too late, that his remark had not only questioned Fleming's efficiency but had also cast doubt on his competence. The air between them cooled, and though Fleming remained composed, the glint in his eye suggested that Mathew had just made an enemy, an enemy who, for now, was bound by duty, but one who would remember this slight.

Clearing his throat, Superintendent Dennis Proud interjected, attempting to ease the moment. "Chief Superintendent Fleming received preliminary reports en route, Your Highness. Standard procedure. Given the nature of the case, our officers began verifying Mr. Clarkson's whereabouts the moment Blair Washington was reported missing."

Mathew inhaled deeply, considering his words more carefully. "I see," he said, his tone softer now. "I didn't mean to imply anything, Chief Superintendent. I was merely surprised by the speed of your confirmation."

Fleming offered a tight nod, the ghost of a smirk at the corner of his lips. "Understood, sir. And for the record, we take these matters very seriously. Every lead, every timeline, every suspect, no matter their title or status, will be scrutinised."

The tension in the room lingered, but the conversation had moved forward. Mathew knew he had misstepped, and while the Chief Superintendent would remain professional, he had just learned a valuable lesson, one did not lightly challenge a seasoned officer of the Metropolitan Police. Callum Gibb had turned his face slightly to hide his grin.

Hugh Drinkwater handed Chief Superintendent Fleming and Inspector Proud his contact number and email address, ensuring a direct line of communication for any case updates. The officers accepted the details with curt nods before excusing themselves, departing the office to presumably resume their investigation. The door clicked shut behind them, leaving Mathew, Callum, and Drinkwater in a moment of shared silence.

As if on cue, all three exchanged glances before rolling their eyes in unison, an unspoken acknowledgment of the rigid formality and barely concealed tension that had just unfolded.

"Well, that went well," Callum muttered dryly, rubbing his temples. "Mathew, you do have a way of making friends in high places."

They all laughed as Drinkwater exhaled sharply, leaning back in his chair his face now composed. "Fleming is sharp, but he's also got a long memory. You may want to tread a little more carefully with him, Your Highness." His tone wasn't admonishing, but it carried a note of caution.

Mathew crossed his arms, exasperated. "I wasn't trying to offend him, I was just surprised at how quickly he had an answer. It felt… premature."

"Maybe," Drinkwater conceded, "but he's not one to bluff. If he says Clarkson has an alibi, he'll have the receipts to back it up." He tapped a finger thoughtfully against his desk. "Still, I wouldn't be so quick to dismiss Clarkson from suspicion. Even if he wasn't directly involved, that doesn't mean he isn't pulling the strings from a distance."

Mathew locked eyes with Drinkwater, his expression unreadable but his voice steady. "What really happened to Roger Pundesh, Hugh? Did you have him killed?"

Drinkwater exhaled slowly, his gaze momentarily dropping to the desk before meeting Mathew's again. "Once we got a lead on him, it unravelled something far bigger than we expected." He leaned forward, resting his elbows on the polished surface. "Serious transactional trading involving highly sensitive royal documents. The internal leaks to Prince Arnold? Minuscule in comparison to what we uncovered."

Callum shifted in his chair, listening intently.

"We had no choice but to hand him over to MI5. From there, he was transferred to the international arm of MI6, where he was interrogated. They wanted names, associates, buyers, the full network." Drinkwater paused for a moment, his expression darkening. "But from what I understand, Pundesh was steadfast. Refused to cooperate."

Mathew's jaw tightened. "So what happened to him?"

Drinkwater's voice was measured, but there was an undertone of resignation. "Apparently, his dealings stretched back years. If even a fraction of what he knew had surfaced, it would have caused deep embarrassment at the highest levels." He sighed, rubbing a hand over his face before glancing up at Mathew and Callum. "It's how they operate, I'm afraid. As one of their men once told me, even if these types of perpetrators are locked in solitary confinement, there's always a risk. Someone, somewhere, hearing something they shouldn't."

A heavy silence filled the room.

Callum exhaled sharply. "So he's gone. Just like that."

Drinkwater didn't answer, but the look in his eyes was enough.

That evening, Mathew received a formal summons from the King for a meeting scheduled the following morning. Though the message was brief and devoid of any indication of urgency, Mathew couldn't shake the feeling that the timing, so soon after the night's troubling events, was significant.

Later that night, as he sat in his suite, he finally placed a call to his mother in Canberra. He had been in London for just over six weeks now, and a pang of guilt struck him for not having reached out sooner. However, his concerns were quickly dismissed.

"Oh, Mathew, darling, don't fret," she assured him, her voice warm yet amused. "I've been getting updates almost daily from the King's office. They've been keeping me quite informed on your progress and development."

Mathew blinked. "My… development?"

"Yes, dear, like a computer program receiving periodic updates," she said with a light chuckle. "It all sounds terribly official, but I must say, it's rather reassuring."

He exhaled, shaking his head with a small laugh. "I suppose that saves me from having to fill in all the details then."

"Not entirely," she teased. "I still expect to hear it from you, not just from some formal report. But tell me, how are you really?"

They spoke for a little while longer, Mathew keeping his answers measured, though he found comfort in hearing her voice. Despite everything happening around him, she was still the one person who made him feel grounded.

By morning, Callum had already taken charge of the preparations for Mathew's audience with the King. Everything had been arranged meticulously, from the timing of his arrival to the finer details of protocol. As he buttoned his cuffs and straightened his jacket, Mathew couldn't help but wonder what awaited him in the King's study.

The King's office was somber as Mathew entered, and he quickly noted the presence of the Queen seated beside her husband. But there was an additional figure in the room, someone who immediately commanded attention: the Chief Constable of The London Metropolitan Police. The Chief was a tall man with a stern face, his presence adding a further layer of tension to the already charged atmosphere.

Mathew was introduced with a polite nod, but he could feel the weight of the moment pressing down on him. After a brief exchange of pleasantries, the King gestured for him to sit.

"In the short period of time that you have been with us, Mathew..." the King began, his voice measured, as if each word was being carefully weighed. He seemed to pause as he mentally calculated the weeks since Mathew's arrival, the briefest flicker of thought before he continued. "Six weeks, I believe it is since your arrival. And in those six weeks, we have seen the discovery of an internal leak that has led to further discoveries of breaches of information. We have witnessed the unfortunate accident of one of our loyal staff members. We have heard whispers of a possible sabotage of avalanche detection equipment, and now, we are painfully aware of the murder of another trusted and loyal employee, Blair Washington."

As the King spoke, Mathew couldn't help but feel the enormity of the situation press upon him. He had become a figurehead for these unfolding events, and though he had tried his best to remain vigilant, it seemed as if the palace itself was drowning in a sea of crises he could barely comprehend. The King paused, his gaze intense as he shifted to lock eyes with Mathew.

"There has not been so much action in the palace since the commencement of the Second World War," the King continued, his tone steely, yet tinged with an underlying frustration. "And now... you've managed to alienate the Chief Superintendent of the Police."

Mathew could feel his heart race. He didn't know where to look, every word from the King felt like a hammer striking against his chest. Despite the pressure, Mathew fought to maintain composure. He wasn't sure what the King expected from him in this moment, but he certainly didn't feel solely responsible for the disasters that seemed to be escalating under his watch.

The silence that followed felt unbearable, as if the weight of the King's words had created a rift between them, one that was impossible to bridge. Just as the tension seemed to thicken in the air, the Queen's voice broke through, sharp and direct, though there was an unexpected warmth to her tone.

"And don't stop, Mathew," she said, her gaze steady, with a subtle encouragement. "However it is that you are bringing these... sunken issues back to the surface... please, do continue."

Her words, though stern, held a sense of curiosity, a desire to understand the full scope of what had transpired. The Queen, who had remained mostly silent up until this point, now seemed to open a small window of understanding for Mathew. The brief encouragement allowed him to breathe a little easier, though the weight of the room still felt unbearable.

The King's stern expression suddenly softened as he took in Mathew's response. A realisation seemed to wash over him, and without missing a beat, his tone shifted from frustration to something else entirely, genuine appreciation. He leaned forward slightly, his voice carrying a new warmth.

"Good God, man!" the King exclaimed, his eyes bright with sudden understanding. "You've been like a breath of fresh air for us. We've been trapped in this suffocating, stifling atmosphere, filled with deceit and corruption for far too long. But by God, you're doing it, you're clearing this air!"

Mathew's shoulders eased slightly at the King's words, though he was still processing the tension that had built up in the room. It was clear that the King had not intended to make him feel like a scapegoat for the palace's troubles, but rather to acknowledge the difficult work Mathew was undertaking. The words felt like a much-needed reprieve after the tense conversation that had unfolded just moments before.

The King's praise was accompanied by a gesture toward the Queen, who now wore a smile of approval, nodding in agreement with her husband's sentiment. Her supportive gaze met Mathew's, offering a subtle but important validation of the King's words.

"You are pushing forward the very changes we've needed," the Queen added, her voice more tempered, but filled with the same encouragement. "We've been tangled in this web for far too long, and it's about time someone had the courage to unravel it."

Mathew felt a flicker of relief as the pressure in the room seemed to lighten. He had braced himself for more criticism, for more scrutiny, but instead, he was met with acknowledgment. It was a small victory, but one that strengthened his resolve.

The King, sensing Mathew's shifting demeanour, leaned back in his chair and continued, his voice carrying a quieter, more thoughtful tone.

"It's easy to forget how suffocating the air has become when you're too close to the problem," he mused. "But you've come from the outside, with fresh eyes and an open mind, and you've done more in these few weeks than we could have hoped for. The work you're doing is difficult, and it's not without its sacrifices. But I truly believe we're on the right path now."

Mathew nodded, a hint of pride beginning to edge its way through the exhaustion that had plagued him since his arrival. There was still much work to be done, countless challenges ahead, but for the first time in what felt like forever, he allowed himself to feel a spark of optimism.

The Chief Constable, having listened attentively to the King and Queen's words of praise, turned his attention to Mathew, his expression sincere and measured. He nodded in approval, then spoke with a tone that blended professionalism and warmth.

"Your Highness," he began, "I must also pass on my commendations. The work you've undertaken here has been nothing short of remarkable. I understand that your approach may differ from what the Chief Superintendent is accustomed to, but I firmly believe that your methods are exactly what we need in these times." He paused, allowing the weight of his words to settle before continuing.

"I do hope that, with a little time, the Chief Superintendent will adjust to your way of working. He's very keen to collaborate with you, and I believe that together, you both can accomplish far more than we could have hoped for in the past. Your fresh perspective is invaluable, Your Highness."

Mathew nodded thoughtfully, appreciating the Chief Constable's candid words. The police force, it seemed, had a vested interest in his approach, and while there were challenges to overcome, particularly with the Chief Superintendent, there was also an underlying sense of collaboration and optimism.

The Chief Constable's next words came with a note of quiet enthusiasm, as if offering a significant opportunity to Mathew.

"If you would like to move your investigative operations to an available office and facility at New Scotland Yard," he suggested, "it would be an honour and a privilege to have you there. We have the space, and I am confident that the resources we can offer will support your efforts as you continue your work here. Consider it an open invitation, Your Highness."

Mathew took a moment to process the offer, impressed by the professionalism and support of the Chief Constable. New Scotland

Yard, with its vast resources and central location, would undoubtedly provide him with the kind of infrastructure he needed to tackle the complex investigations that had unfolded since his arrival. It was an enticing proposal, but also one that required careful consideration.

"Thank you, Chief Constable," Mathew said, his voice measured but sincere. "I will certainly consider your offer and discuss it with my staff. It's an opportunity that warrants serious thought, and I appreciate your support in making it available to us."

The Chief Constable gave a respectful nod, clearly pleased with Mathew's response. "Of course, Your Highness. I look forward to hearing your decision. Should you choose to take us up on the offer, know that we will do everything in our power to ensure your success."

Mathew felt a quiet sense of gratitude toward the Chief Constable. Despite the tension surrounding the investigation, it was clear that the police were eager to work alongside him, offering both their expertise and their resources. It was a partnership that could prove invaluable in the days to come and when Mathew mentioned it to Hugh Drinkwater he suggested that we jump at the offer of their facilities.

Blair Washington's funeral was a solemn and deeply moving affair. Though Mathew had not known him for long, he felt the weight of his passing more than he had expected. It was not just the loss of a valued colleague but of a friend he had barely begun to know, one whose kindness, loyalty, and dedication had left a lasting impression.

The ceremony was understated yet dignified, a reflection of the man Blair had been. Close friends, family, and colleagues gathered to pay their final respects, their grief palpable in the hushed whispers and bowed heads. A somber air settled over the congregation as heartfelt eulogies were delivered, each one painting a picture of a man who had been deeply respected and dearly loved.

Mathew remained largely incognito throughout the service, standing quietly at the back of the chapel, observing the proceedings with a heavy heart. He was recognised by only a few of Blair's closest colleagues, those who had worked alongside him in the palace. Though they acknowledged him with brief nods, none approached him directly, either out of deference or their own sorrow.

As the service concluded and the mourners slowly filed out, Mathew lingered for a moment, lost in thought. Blair's untimely death was not just a tragedy but a stark reminder of the dangers lurking beneath the surface. This was no ordinary loss, it was a calculated act, a consequence of the tangled web of deceit they were only beginning to unravel.

He exhaled slowly, his jaw tightening with quiet resolve. There would be justice for Blair Washington. And Mathew intended to see it through.

That evening, after the light dinner that was put on at Rubens Bar at the Palace Hotel for Blair's fellow workmates, Mathew and Callum found themselves in the quiet ambience of the palace bar, sharing drinks and reminiscing about Blair. They laughed softly as they recalled Blair's hopeless attempts at playing snooker, his competitive spirit never quite matching his skill. The mood was bittersweet, fond memories tinged with the undeniable sadness of his absence.

As Callum took a sip of his drink, Mathew's gaze wandered across the room and landed on a white baby grand piano tucked into the corner by the lounge. He hadn't noticed it when he had first entered earlier. Something about it called to him. Without a word, he rose from his seat and strolled over, lifting the lid and propping it open. He slid onto the stool, raised the keyboard cover, and, without much thought, began to play In My Life by The Beatles. The melancholic melody filled the room, a quiet tribute to Blair, though Mathew hadn't consciously intended it as such.

Callum, intrigued, walked over with their drinks just as Mathew transitioned seamlessly into Wish You Were Here by Pink Floyd. The song choice, whether deliberate or not, struck a chord with those present. The soft murmur of conversation died down as people took notice. The gentle notes carried across the room, drawing staff members from adjoining lounges and corridors, one by one drifting closer to see what was happening.

Taking a brief pause to sip his drink, Mathew set the glass down and, with a glint of mischief in his eye, launched into Honky Tonk Women by The Rolling Stones. The sudden shift in tempo caught everyone by surprise. Heads turned. Smiles spread. Feet began tapping. By then, Mathew was lost in the music, unable to stop himself. One song flowed into another, an impromptu concert unfolding in the most unexpected of places.

Unbeknownst to him, the King and Queen had made an unannounced visit to the bar, intending to pay their respects to those staff members still mourning Blair. Instead, they found themselves standing at the entrance, watching in astonishment as Mathew, completely absorbed, continued to play with an ease and passion neither of them had ever witnessed before.

The King, raising an eyebrow, exchanged a look with the Queen, who simply smiled. "Well," he murmured under his breath, "I certainly didn't see this coming."

The following morning, Mathew and Callum made their way to Blair Washington's office in the palace. The air inside was heavy with absence, the space still held Blair's presence in the form of neatly stacked papers, half-finished notes, and the faint scent of his cologne lingering in the air.

They had come to retrieve the files and documents Blair had been compiling on Corvatsch, an investigation that had consumed much of his final days. Mathew moved to the desk, running his hand lightly over its polished surface before opening the top drawer. Inside, precisely where Blair had left it, was a thick dossier.

Callum picked up a file from the stack on the side table, flipping it open. "Here it is," he said, tapping the cover with his fingers. "Bruno Eckart, Corvatsch Avalanche Monitoring Centre."

Dossier: Bruno Eckart

Age: 29
Former Position: Avalanche Analyst, Corvatsch Avalanche Monitoring Centre (CAMC)
Specialisation: Ground-level snow analysis, including snow depth, density, and movement tracking

Background & Career at CAMC:

Bruno Eckart was the youngest member of the Corvatsch Avalanche Monitoring Centre team, a rising talent in the field of alpine meteorology and snow behaviour analysis. Originally from Innsbruck, Austria, Eckart developed a fascination with mountainous terrain from a young age, growing up in a family of avid skiers and climbers. He pursued a degree in Geophysical Sciences at ETH Zurich, where he focused his research on the shifting patterns of snowfall and avalanche prediction.

Joining CAMC at 26, Eckart was assigned to ground-level snow analysis, a critical role in avalanche risk assessment. His work involved measuring snowpack depth, density, and movement, ensuring that data from field studies aligned with satellite and

Max Barrington

drone-based observations. Considered highly intelligent but somewhat introverted, Eckart was known for his meticulous attention to detail, until discrepancies in his reports raised concerns.

Concerns & Missing Data:

In the months leading up to the Corvatsch Avalanche Disaster, irregularities began surfacing in Eckart's logs. Observations were incomplete or missing on key nights, particularly during periods of heavy snowfall when real-time monitoring was crucial. His absence during critical shifts became a point of contention among his colleagues, with some questioning his reliability and work ethic.

Following the avalanche that claimed multiple lives, an internal review of CAMC's records found that Eckart had failed to log significant snow buildup data in the days leading to the disaster. This omission raised the possibility that early warnings may have been missed or ignored. Attempts to locate him immediately after the incident proved difficult, as he had quietly resigned from his position and left Corvatsch.

Notes attached to the file from Blair;

Eckart's departure was sudden. Within a week of the avalanche, he had formally submitted his resignation, citing personal reasons. He relocated to Geneva, where he reportedly took up short-term consultancy work in environmental risk management. However, his low profile and reluctance to speak to former colleagues or investigators added to suspicions about his potential involvement in, or knowledge of, failures within CAMC's monitoring system.

Rumours persist that Eckart may have been pressured into suppressing data or that he was aware of larger systemic failures within the organisation. Some speculate that he was either a scapegoat for negligence or complicit in a cover-up. His current whereabouts remain unclear, and there are indications that he may have connections with external entities interested in avalanche research data for undisclosed purposes.

Key Questions?

Why were Eckart's logs incomplete in the weeks leading up to the disaster?

Did he intentionally suppress data, or was it negligence?

Why did he abruptly resign and distance himself from CAMC?

Was he acting alone, or was he influenced by external forces?

Gossip of Eckhart and Von Hohenfels in a relationship? But Eckhart is married and they have one small child??

Here ended Blairs notes:

As they were about to leave with the file, Hugh Drinkwater entered the office, his sharp eyes immediately catching sight of the dossier in Callum's hand.

"Ah, precisely what I came here for," he remarked, striding forward. Without hesitation, he reached for the file. "I'll make you a copy," he added, taking it from Callum's grasp.

It was only then that he noticed Mathew standing just behind Callum. Straightening slightly, he greeted him with a respectful nod. "Good morning, Your Highness," he said. "I intend to begin a thorough investigation into this, as well as the entire CAMC staff report, using Scotland Yard's facilities today."

Mathew's expression sharpened with interest. "Excellent!" he responded without hesitation. "We'll join you."

Drinkwater arched a brow, momentarily surprised, before offering a small, knowing smile. "I expected nothing less," he replied.

The facilities allocated to the palace security team at Scotland Yard were second to none, offering state-of-the-art resources, dedicated personnel, and seamless integration with international agencies such as Interpol. Secure communication lines, extensive databases, and an advanced file-sharing system allowed for near-instant access to critical intelligence, capabilities that would have once required bureaucratic red tape and lengthy application processes.

Hugh Drinkwater could hardly contain his enthusiasm as he stood alongside Mathew and Callum, all three of them poring over the Bruno Eckhart file. "This is incredible," he said, almost to himself. "The ease with which we can now access files and information, things we used to wait weeks for, is nothing short of a game-changer."

Mathew, still focused on the investigation at hand, glanced up from the documents. "Can we get a copy of Marta Von Hohenfels' records?" he asked. His tone was calm but firm, the request carrying the weight of necessity.

Drinkwater looked thoughtful for a moment, then nodded. "I'll see what I can do," he replied. "If there's anything on her in the system, we'll have it soon enough." In a few moments the printer on the desk ejected the dossier;

Dossier: Marta Von Hohenfels

Full Name: Marta Ingrid Von Hohenfels
Age: 30
Nationality: Swiss
Occupation: Administrative Officer, Corvatsch Avalanche Monitoring Centre (CAMC)
Years at CAMC: 2

Background & Professional Role:

Marta Von Hohenfels joined the Corvatsch Avalanche Monitoring Centre (CAMC) two years ago as the station's administrative officer. Unlike the other members of the team, she does not have a technical or scientific background in meteorology or snow analysis. Instead, her responsibilities focus on handling official reports, coordinating with cantonal authorities, maintaining operational records, and ensuring compliance with safety regulations.

Colleagues described her as efficient, detail-oriented, and highly professional, though some noted she kept a degree of personal distance from the rest of the team. Despite her non-technical role, she had access to internal reports and monitoring data, giving her insight into the daily workings of the station.

Connection to Bruno Eckhart:

Frequent Interactions: Despite working in different areas, Von Hohenfels and Eckhart were observed spending an unusual amount of time together. Some colleagues remarked that Eckhart, who was known for being somewhat unreliable in his record-keeping, would often rely on Von Hohenfels to "fix" discrepancies in his logs.

Unrecorded Meetings: Staff noted that Von Hohenfels and Eckhart often spoke privately, sometimes in the records room or outside the main station. While these meetings could have been work-related, the secrecy surrounding them raised suspicions.

Co-ordinated Absences: A review of station logs revealed that both Von Hohenfels and Eckhart were absent on key nights when crucial snowfall data should have been reviewed. While their absences were separately documented, the overlapping timeframes suggest they may have left together.

Von Hohenfels was not on duty the day of the avalanche, however, Dr. Anya Keller, had reported, possibly, seeing her with Eckhart on that night at the detonator store. She is not certain of this sighting and she may be confused.

Witness Testimonies: A few staff members reported seeing Von Hohenfels and Eckhart arriving at the station together in the mornings, even when their shifts did not align. On one occasion, a staff member allegedly overheard an argument between the two regarding an "unnecessary risk" Eckhart had taken.

Behaviour After the Avalanche: Following the Corvatsch avalanche, Von Hohenfels was noticeably distressed and took an unexpected leave of absence soon after Eckhart resigned. While she claimed this was due to personal reasons, some speculated that her departure was linked to Eckhart's sudden exit.

Conclusion:

While there is no direct evidence proving a romantic relationship between Von Hohenfels and Eckhart, the nature of their interactions, unexplained absences, and her reaction following the avalanche suggest a personal connection beyond a standard working relationship. Given Von Hohenfels' access to operational records and her ability to modify official reports, further investigation is necessary to determine whether she played a role in covering for Eckhart or whether their association influenced key decisions leading up to the avalanche.

Once again, all three men stood shoulder to shoulder at the large table, their eyes scanning the contents of the report before them. The air was thick with unspoken tension, each of them waiting for the other to make the first move.

"Let's start, shall we?" Mathew finally said, breaking the silence. His voice carried an air of quiet authority, one that left no room for hesitation. He had grown increasingly impatient with the stagnant deliberations, particularly with Drinkwater's tendency to either state the obvious or make comments that, in Mathew's view, contributed little to their progress.

Enough was enough. If Drinkwater was going to be of use, he needed to prove it now. Otherwise, Mathew was prepared to shake the proverbial tree and let Drinkwater fall from it entirely. They had work to do, real work, and Mathew was determined that they would not simply stand around passively, allowing valuable time to slip away while their investigation remained at a standstill.

"Man the whiteboard, Drinkie!" Mathew called out, tossing a marker in Hugh Drinkwater's direction. It clattered against the whiteboard tray before Drinkwater caught it with an awkward fumble. "Right,... write this down, at the very top, we have our perceived 'top minion', no, don't write that, Hugh. Not 'top minion', write 'Clarkson.'" Mathew leaned forward, resting his hands on the table. "Now, we all believe he's at the top of this somewhere, yeah?"

     Max Barrington

"We... don't know that for sure at this stage," Drinkwater objected cautiously. "I mean, there's no actual evidence."

Mathew inhaled sharply, clenching his jaw. He could feel his patience stretching dangerously thin.

"I fucking know that, Drinkie," he snapped, his frustration boiling over. "This isn't a damn courtroom, so don't start defending people. I'm trying to establish some sort of order here, some kind of framework we can work with. And if you don't think you can contribute in a constructive way, then I strongly suggest you piss off now."

He let the words hang in the air for a moment before doubling down.

"Yes, piss off now, Drinkie. Go back to your office and pretend to do something."

The room fell into a stunned silence. For a moment, Drinkwater just stood there, his face unreadable. Then, without a word, he removed his security pass for Scotland Yard, placed it deliberately on the table, and walked out.

The three female assistants in the office kept their eyes down, pretending to be absorbed in their work, but the tension was thick enough to cut with a knife.

Mathew exhaled sharply, running a hand through his hair. Then, regathering himself, he clapped his hands together and turned to Callum.

"Now," he said, his voice steadier but still laced with irritation, "let's get something started before we all die of old age."

Without another word, he strode toward the door, intent on finding the HR officer. They needed a replacement, someone sharp, someone who could keep up. It was time to bring in a 'super sleuth.' One of the assistants gave Mathew directions to Chief Inspector Angelo Villani, the human resources officer at Scotland Yard.

"The only 'super sleuths' we have are already out working cases, Your Highness," Angelo said, leaning back in his chair. "We've got an acute shortage of highly intelligent officers, and recruiting is going full throttle just to keep up."

He sighed, rubbing the bridge of his nose before continuing. "The Metropolitan Police Service, covering the whole of Greater London, is one of the largest police forces in the world, with a budget exceeding £17 billion. And yet, despite all that, we're struggling to maintain our numbers. We're short by at least 2,500 officers and staff." He shook his head. "Yes, 2,500 men and women down."

As he spoke, Angelo moved toward the sleek DeLonghi coffee machine sitting on a side table. "Cappuccino?" He gestured toward the machine.

Mathew, still absorbing the dire state of affairs, gave a slight nod. "Sure."

Angelo pressed a few buttons, and the machine whirred to life, filling the room with the rich aroma of freshly brewed coffee. "One of the biggest reasons for the shortfall," he continued, "is inadequate funding. We've been hit with government budget cuts year after year, which has squeezed our resources and made it damn near impossible to recruit and retain officers."

He handed Mathew a cappuccino and took a sip of his own before going on. "It's not just the budget, though. The job itself isn't attracting people like it used to. Salaries are low, job security is shaky, and frankly, a lot of young people don't see the appeal of signing up for a career where they're overworked, underpaid, and constantly in high-stress situations."

Angelo leaned against the counter, shaking his head again. "Can you blame them? Long hours, physical demands, and a lifetime of dealing with crime, corruption, and bureaucracy... all for a pay packet that barely competes with what they could get in the private sector. Most of them look at policing and say, 'No thanks, there are easier ways to make a living.'"

Mathew exhaled slowly, his fingers tapping lightly against the side of his coffee cup. The weight of the situation settled on him, Scotland Yard was stretched thin, and if they were hoping for any significant support, they'd be waiting a long time. If this case was going to be solved, it would have to be on their own terms, with whatever resources they could scrape together.

Angelo must have sensed his frustration because he gave a knowing smirk and leaned in slightly. "But," he said, his voice carrying a hint of amusement, "I do have a young lad here we've been putting through some additional training. He's a bit… let's just say he's got a few handicaps."

Mathew raised an eyebrow, intrigued but skeptical.

"He's soft," Angelo continued. "A little slow in certain ways. But don't let that fool you, he's sharp. Smart as hell, actually. The problem is, he never stops asking questions. You'll barely get a word in before he's firing off another one. It drives some of the older detectives mad."

Mathew took another sip of his coffee, considering the offer.

"But he's honest," Angelo added, as if that was the real selling point. "And in our line of work, that counts for a hell of a lot. If you want him, you can have him for as long as you need. He might surprise you."

Mathew studied Angelo for a moment, then gave a slight nod. "Alright. We'll take him."

"Good," Angelo said, turning toward his desk. "Finish your coffee, I'll send for him now."

Mathew introduced Constable 24324, Adrian Harrison, to Callum and the three office assistants, Senior Constable Julie Coogan, Senior Constable Susan Reynolds, and Sergeant Nicole Evans. "Adrian is going to be our chief detective on this case, and I want everyone to give him your full support." His tone left no room for debate; he needed a team that worked together seamlessly.

As Mathew turned his attention to the whiteboard, he noticed that in his absence, Nicole had taken the initiative to start organising their leads. At the top of the board was the name Clarkson, the presumed mastermind, or at least the highest-ranking individual they suspected. Beneath him were Aldrich Müller, Marta von Hohenfels, and Bruno Eckhart, all figures tangled within the growing web of intrigue.

Adrian, standing beside him, studied the names with a furrowed brow before asking, "Who are these people?" His voice carried a particular cadence, one Mathew couldn't immediately place but felt strangely familiar.

He dismissed the thought at first, but as the day wore on, he found himself increasingly drawn to the distinct tone of Adrian's speech. There was something deliberate about it, something methodical. Then, like a sudden bolt of recognition, it clicked, Adrian's way of speaking reminded him of a childhood friend from school, a boy who had Asperger's syndrome.

That friend had possessed a relentless curiosity, asking endless questions about everything, often fixating on details others would overlook. Mathew's mother had once given him a piece of advice about handling those interactions: Reverse the flow, answer a question with a question. Let them engage in their own thought process by making them think through the answer.

The realisation brought a small smile to Mathew's face as he approached Adrian with a measured pace. "These names on the board, Adrian," he began, keeping his tone even, "as Callum mentioned earlier, these are the individuals we believe may have had some influence over the avalanche that claimed the lives of the ruling monarch and his family."

He paused, sensing Adrian's need to process the information. True to expectation, Adrian took the opportunity to voice his thoughts on the tragedy, his words laced with genuine sorrow, particularly for the children who had perished. Mathew listened patiently as Adrian expressed his heartfelt sympathy, his words stretching on longer than expected. Still, Mathew knew better than to interrupt.

Once it seemed Adrian had concluded his thoughts, Mathew smoothly guided the conversation forward. "Now, I suggest we go through each of these individuals, those listed on the whiteboard. We'll start with their position profiles within the Corvatsch Avalanche Monitoring Centre and then move on to their dossiers."

Barely a second passed before Adrian interjected, his expression focused. "Clarkson wasn't employed by CAMC."

Mathew felt Callum stiffen beside him, his coat sleeve twitching slightly as if he were about to step in. But before Callum could say a word, Mathew caught the fabric between his fingers, just a light tug. A silent message: It's fine. Let it go. Patience.

Turning back to Adrian, Mathew met his gaze with a knowing smile. "You're absolutely right, Adrian," he acknowledged, his voice steady. "Clarkson wasn't with CAMC. So, let's start with the ones who were."

As he spoke, he cast a quick glance around the room, catching the subtle smirks and barely restrained amusement of the others. It was going to take some time to adjust to Adrian's meticulous nature, but Mathew was already beginning to appreciate the way his mind worked.

After a few minutes of silence, Adrian suddenly looked up from the dossier he was reading and turned to Mathew. "Mathew," he asked, his face completely serious, "are you really a Prince?"

The question caught everyone off guard, and a burst of laughter rippled through the room. Even Callum, who had been intently studying one of the files, let out a chuckle. Mathew, amused but unfazed, leaned back slightly.

"That's what they tell me," he replied dryly, before nodding toward the whiteboard. "Now, Adrian, you had another question?"

"Yes," Adrian continued, seemingly unfazed by the reaction. "Why are the names in this order?"

Mathew was quick to turn the question back on him. "Why do you think they're in that order, Adrian?"

Adrian frowned slightly, considering the question. "I have no idea," he admitted, shaking his head. "But it's wrong."

Everyone in the room turned their attention to him now, curiosity piqued. Adrian stood, walked over to the whiteboard, and, without hesitation, adjusted the arrangement of the names.

The new order now read:

Clarkson (unchanged)

Hohenfels (moved up)

Müller

Eckhart

He stepped back and crossed his arms. "That makes more sense."

Mathew raised an eyebrow. "Why?"

"Because," Adrian explained, "if we're ranking them by status and potential influence, Marta Von Hohenfels should be second, not Müller. She had direct access to administrative records, communication channels, and decision-making processes. Müller was perhaps high-ranking in the chain of things, but in this case, I think he was more of a technical figure, not a gatekeeper of information. Eckhart, the youngest and least experienced, belongs at the bottom, he is the vulnerable one, the one that has been used in my opinion."

A quiet murmur of understanding swept through the room. Callum glanced at Mathew, nodding slightly.

Before anyone could comment further, Adrian continued, "We should also check their bank accounts, all the staff bank accounts. We are looking for any unusual transactions might tell us more about who was really pulling the strings."

Mathew turned to Julie. "Get on that now, payroll records, bank details, anything we can legally access."

                                        Max Barrington

Julie gave a quick nod and left to make the calls. As she disappeared through the door, all eyes turned back to Adrian, waiting for his next insight.

Instead, Adrian smiled, glanced at the clock, and casually announced, "It's my lunchtime."

A beat of silence. Then, Callum exhaled a short laugh while Mathew rubbed his temple. The room, momentarily tense with deep analysis, was now laced with unexpected amusement.

Julie had been efficient in her task, swiftly retrieving all the bank account information from the paymaster records at CAMC. Through subsequent contacts with the relevant banks, facilitated via Interpol, she had managed to obtain detailed bank statements covering the past three months up to the present day.

As the team sifted through the records, scanning for any irregularities, one account immediately stood out. Marta Von Hohenfels' financial activity raised more than a few eyebrows, her Credit Suisse account, registered at Via Maistra 14 in St. Moritz, showed an uncharacteristically large cash deposit of SFr150,000.

Mathew leaned in closer, his gaze narrowing as he examined the statement. "That's not a regular pay packet," he murmured, tapping his finger against the figure.

Callum let out a low whistle. "That's a hell of a lot of money to show up out of nowhere."

Adrian, who had been quietly observing the discussion, tilted his head. "When exactly was the deposit made?"

Julie scanned the details. "Two weeks before the avalanche."

The room fell silent for a moment as the weight of that information settled over them. Mathew finally exhaled sharply. "That's either one hell of a coincidence... or we just found our first real lead." Everyone was in high spirits. It had been a productive day, and the breakthrough that afternoon felt like a significant step forward. There was an undeniable energy in the room, a sense that they were finally gaining traction in the case.

Adrian, ever pragmatic, gave Mathew a casual thumbs-up as he shrugged into his coat. "What time tomorrow?" he asked, already halfway to the door.

Mathew checked his watch, slightly taken aback by the question. "Uh, same time as today, I suppose, "

But Adrian had already nodded in acknowledgment, opened the door, and was gone.

Susan let out a small chuckle, shaking her head in amusement. "Now there's a man who doesn't take work home with him."

Julie, still glancing at the now-closed door, smiled. "There goes one very smart man," she agreed. "In more ways than one."

Mathew exhaled, rubbing his chin thoughtfully. "Bugger," he muttered. "I reckon we could have uncovered more if we pushed on a little longer. But I don't want Adrian missing anything, especially after a debut like today."

Callum grinned. "Don't worry, Mathew. Something tells me he'll be back tomorrow with more questions than we have answers for."

Mathew smirked. "Yeah. And I have a feeling we'll be needing every single one of them."

Jigsaw Puzzle

Mathew dined with the King that evening at the Palace, and as the night went on, he found himself truly enjoying the royal lifestyle.

There was an effortless grandeur to it all, fine dining, impeccable service, and the company of a monarch who, despite his status, was refreshingly conversational. He found himself hoping that this bubble of privilege would never burst.

As they sat over their meal, the King suddenly asked, "Do you like hunting, Mathew?"

It was an unexpected question, one that caught Mathew slightly off guard. He took a moment before replying. "Contrary to popular belief, sir, not all Australians are good at horse riding." He figured it was better to be honest than to pretend he was some sort of outback horseman.

The King raised an eyebrow before breaking into a short chuckle. "What on earth has horse riding got to do with hunting? I meant shotgunning, game birds, mostly. We walk, Mathew, we don't ride horses. Good lord, no."

Mathew immediately realised his mistake. He had assumed the King was referring to traditional fox hunting, the aristocratic image of red coats, hounds, and galloping through the countryside. The King seemed to recognise the misunderstanding as well.

"You're probably thinking of fox hunting, my boy," he continued, swirling the wine in his glass. "No, we don't do that anymore, too many activists campaigning against it, insisting it's cruel or that the foxes deserve to be saved." He took a sip of his drink before exhaling, lost in thought. "A shame, really. It's a centuries-old British tradition. But people these days, many of them, I suspect, become activists simply for the sake of activism. They take a stand against things without truly understanding what they're protesting."

Mathew listened intently as the King leaned back slightly, his voice taking on a more reflective tone. "They call it cruelty, yet they have little regard for what the fox does in the wild. They never seem to consider the slow, agonising death of a newborn lamb when a fox gets hold of it. The lamb's mother bleats helplessly, unable to save her offspring. But no one protests that, do they?"

Mathew nodded thoughtfully, recognising the King's frustration. It was an old-world perspective clashing with modern sensibilities, a recurring theme among those who had lived through changing times. He decided to tread carefully with his response, knowing this was more than just a discussion about hunting.

"I'll tell you a story," the King said, a wry smile playing at the corners of his mouth. "Something one of my uncles told me years ago. It's about an activist group, a rather determined bunch of ladies, who decided to attend a farmers' meeting. Now, this wasn't just any meeting; it was being held to organise a large-scale fox drive, a co-ordinated cull to control the fox population and protect livestock."

Mathew leaned in slightly, intrigued. The King took another sip of his drink before continuing.

"The activist group had sent a speaker, a well-meaning but thoroughly misguided woman, who took the floor and addressed the farmers. She made an impassioned plea, arguing that rather than expending so much effort on a cull, the farmers should instead focus on capturing the foxes. Her grand solution?" The King's voice took on a bemused edge. "She proposed that instead of killing them, they should release all the female foxes and, here's the best part, castrate all the males before setting them free again."

Mathew suppressed a chuckle but said nothing, waiting for the punchline he could already sense was coming.

"The farmers, being polite country folk, respectfully listened to the activist's suggestion without interruption. They let her finish her speech, nodded along, and allowed her to have her say." The King leaned in slightly, his smile widening. "And then, when she was done, one of the older farmers stood up, removed his hat, and addressed her with the utmost sincerity."

The King paused for dramatic effect before delivering the farmer's response.

"'Madam,' he said, 'I do believe you don't quite understand. The foxes aren't shagging the lambs. They're killing them.'"

Mathew let out a bark of laughter, unable to hold it in any longer. The King grinned, clearly pleased with the reaction.

"And that," the King added, "is the problem with a great many activists. They mean well, but they don't always take the time to understand what they're actually protesting."

Mathew nodded, still chuckling. "That's a hell of a story, sir."

The King raised his glass. "That it is, my boy. That it is."

It was a rather splendid night, one of those rare evenings where everything felt just right. The conversation had been engaging, the setting opulent yet comfortable, and Mathew found himself truly savouring the time spent with his father. These moments were becoming increasingly precious to him, a realisation that settled deep in his chest.

As the night drew to a close, Callum, ever the reliable presence, was already seated in the car that would take him back to the house where he had been staying. He had grown quite comfortable there, and Mathew suspected that, despite his grumbling, Callum secretly enjoyed the luxury.

Before retiring for the night, Mathew and Callum made their way to the bar for a final drink. The quiet hum of the palace settling for the evening, the clink of crystal against polished wood, and the faint aroma of aged whiskey in the air made for a moment of perfect calm. They perched on the bar stools, chatting idly about the coming day at Scotland Yard, exchanging thoughts on the investigation with a relaxed ease.

Then, the shrill buzz of Mathew's mobile phone cut through the tranquility.

Without hesitation, Callum slid off his stool and moved to the opposite side of the bar, giving Mathew the privacy to take his call. It was an unspoken understanding between them, one that came from the familiarity of working together. Some conversations were best kept private, and Callum, ever perceptive, knew better than to linger.

Mathew took a slow breath, steeling himself before answering. Whatever this was, he had a feeling the night wasn't quite over yet.

"Well, have you been so busy that you haven't had time to call me back?" Rhianna's voice came through the phone, smooth but with an edge that Mathew couldn't ignore. She was Mathew's girlfriend, or perhaps ex-girlfriend, as he'd been thinking more frequently in recent days.

"I didn't think you wanted me to call you back," Mathew replied, his tone guarded. The last conversation they'd had left him feeling more exhausted than anything else, and now he found himself wondering why he ever felt so honoured by her attention.

Rhianna's voice softened, attempting to sound sincere. "Is it true?"

Mathew braced himself, already knowing what was coming. "Is what true?" he asked, trying to sound indifferent, though part of him already felt a knot form in his stomach.

"That you're now 'Prince Mathew,' and heir to the throne?" Her voice was silky, but there was a hint of amusement in it, a clear attempt to draw him into her world of shallow curiosity. Mathew rolled his eyes, sensing the transparency of her act. It was almost sickening how obvious she was trying to sound interested.

Without missing a beat, Mathew decided to cut through the pretentiousness. "Yes, that is all true," he said evenly, his tone devoid of the warmth or eagerness she might have once drawn from him. "You must drop by the next time you're in London. Goodbye."

He ended the call without hesitation, exhaling as he set the phone down. A strange mix of relief and irritation settled over him, relief because he no longer had to endure her insincere curiosity, and irritation because she had even bothered to call in the first place. It was as if he had just turned the final page on a chapter that had long outlived its relevance.

Besides, he simply didn't have time for distractions. His life had become a whirlwind of obligations, responsibilities, and a future he had never quite envisioned for himself. Time was slipping through his fingers, each day consumed by meetings, strategic discussions, and the overwhelming task he had taken on.

His father and stepmother had entrusted him with a formidable charter, one aimed at rooting out corruption and dismantling the layers of crime that had quietly embedded themselves within the royal framework. It was an immense challenge, but Mathew had never been one to shy away from difficult tasks. The weight of expectation pressed on his shoulders, but he welcomed it.

There were far more pressing matters at hand than entertaining an ex-girlfriend's sudden and self-serving interest.

Mathew had received a call from Adrian Harrison, but the way it had reached him was nothing short of a bureaucratic relay. The message had first passed through the Chief Constable, then Chief Superintendent Neville Fleming, followed by Chief Inspector Angelo Villani, before finally landing in Mathew's hands. By the time Adrian's voice came through the line, his frustration was palpable.

"This is Adrian, Mathew! This is ridiculous, it's taken me almost an entire day just to get through to you. We need to sort out a better system for communication."

At first, Mathew was taken aback by the audacity of the caller's tone. A mere constable, addressing him in the same manner a king might be spoken to? That was not going to fly. However, as Adrian continued speaking, Mathew found himself reassessing his initial reaction.

It became clear that Adrian wasn't being deliberately insolent; rather, his mind operated in a way that saw Mathew not as an untouchable royal figure but simply as another person, perhaps a boss, but ultimately just another individual in the working world. And when Mathew thought about it, how exactly did one go about contacting a royal prince?

Adrian had likely been forced to climb the ranks of command, starting with his sergeant and painstakingly working his way up the chain of senior officers until his request was finally deemed worthy of passing through. By the time he reached Mathew, he had every reason to be exasperated.

Mathew couldn't help but smirk at the absurdity of it all. Clearly, if he was going to be effective in his new role, he needed to rethink how people, especially those directly involved in important matters, could get in touch with him.

"Sorry Adrian, I shall get something organised today and you will be the first to know, what is it that you need to contact for?"

It was a long story, and listening to its drawn-out details required patience. Adrian had been rostered onto general duties the previous night, an assignment that, in hindsight, seemed to have been a mistake.

While on patrol, Adrian and his partner, Senior Constable Cheryl Thomas, noticed a car driving erratically. It was a BMW M60 with German number plates, weaving unpredictably through traffic. They signalled for the driver to pull over and conducted a routine breath test. The result was staggering, 62 micrograms of alcohol per 100 millilitres of breath, nearly twice the legal limit of 35. With that reading, there was no question: the driver was over the limit and had to be taken to Finsbury Park Police Station for a formal breath analysis test.

Once at the station, standard procedure required the driver to produce his license. At first glance, his name meant nothing to Adrian. But after a few moments, something clicked, the surname Müller. A common enough name, much like Miller in English, but there was something about it that nagged at him. Then, as his eyes moved over the license, the first name, Aldrich, triggered another memory. He had seen that name recently.

It took only a moment for it to come rushing back, the whiteboard at Scotland Yard. The avalanche case in Switzerland. An Aldrich Müller, had been connected to that investigation. Of course, there could be plenty of people with the same name, but this one wasn't just anyone. This Aldrich Müller had a German-registered vehicle, and his listed address? Suvretta, Chasellas, St. Moritz. That was no coincidence.

As Adrian examined the license, he casually asked the man where he was from. Müller confirmed the address without hesitation. "A long, long way from here, mein Herr," Adrian had remarked, watching for any reaction.

But that wasn't the end of it. Having failed both the breath analysis test and a drug test, protocol required a mandatory search of the man's personal belongings and his vehicle. What they found changed everything.

Tucked away among his possessions was a stash of 120 grams of amphetamine, enough to raise serious questions about his intentions. And then there was the discovery that set alarm bells ringing. Hidden under the cover of the spare wheel, taped securely in place, was a dvd.

The contents of the dvd initially suggested it might be a pornographic film. As per protocol, the arresting officers needed to confirm its nature before handing it over to forensics for classification. It took only a brief glimpse of the footage for Adrian to recognise something, or rather, someone, that made his stomach tighten.

Among the participants in the film, one figure stood out immediately. The face, the posture, the subtle mannerisms, it all bore an unsettling resemblance to Bruno Eckhart.

Adrian's pulse quickened. That face had been identified once before, captured in the grainy security footage from the Hotel Steffani in Switzerland. Dr. Meinhardt, the principal of the CAMC (Corvatsch Avalanche Monitoring Control), had positively identified Eckhart as a former employee of the organisation. And now, here he was again, appearing in an explicit recording found in the vehicle of an intoxicated driver with links to Switzerland.

Adrian had no idea who the woman in the film was, but he knew one thing, this DVD needed closer examination. Wasting no time, he arranged for forensic technicians to extract high-resolution screenshots from the footage, isolating key frames featuring Eckhart and his unidentified companion. He now had two names that had appeared on the whiteboard and this was the reason for his call.

Mathew was astonished, not just by the sheer weight of the information Adrian had uncovered, but by the way he had pieced it all together and managed to get through the bureaucratic maze to reach him. What a legend, Mathew thought.

"Adrian, I'll see you in our office at Scotland Yard first thing tomorrow morning. Thanks again!" Mathew said, his appreciation evident.

As he hung up the phone in his room, his mind was already racing ahead. This case was evolving fast, and they needed to streamline communication if they were going to stay ahead of it. He immediately called for Callum.

"Callum, I need you to get six modern iPhones, top of the line," Mathew instructed. "One for me, one for you, and one each for Constable Adrian Harrison, Senior Constable Julie Coogan, Senior Constable Susan Reynolds, and Sergeant Nicole Evans."

Callum nodded, already anticipating the reasoning behind the request.

"Make sure every number is programmed into all of them. From here on out, we operate as a direct unit, no delays, no middlemen. I don't want another situation where it takes a full day for urgent information to reach me."

Callum gave a curt nod of understanding before stepping out to make it happen. Mathew exhaled, running a hand through his hair. If Adrian's discovery was any indication, things were about to get a whole lot more complicated. And he needed his team to be ready.

The next morning, on their way to Scotland Yard, Mathew took the opportunity to bring Callum up to speed on Adrian's late-night revelations. Callum, ever the strategist, listened intently, his expression shifting from curiosity to keen interest. By the time they arrived at headquarters, he was just as eager as the rest of the team to hear the full report.

Inside the briefing room, Adrian wasted no time. He stood before the whiteboard, methodically laying out the key details. Two photographs were now pinned up, each matched with a name, Aldrich Müller and Bruno Eckhart. Both men were now more than just names on a file; they were faces in an emerging web of connections.

But there was more. Adrian had also extracted a facial image from the dvd, the woman who had appeared alongside Eckhart. He placed her photo beside the others, securing it to the board with a magnet. Then, in a deliberate motion, he picked up a marker, drew a bold question mark beneath her image, and connected it with a line to the name Marta Von Hohenfels.

The room fell silent for a moment as everyone processed what they were seeing.

Mathew narrowed his eyes. "Are we certain?" he asked, his voice level but charged with meaning.

Adrian exhaled, running a hand through his hair. "Not yet," he admitted. "But I took the liberty of forwarding the photograph to Dr. Meinhardt at the CAMC. We're just waiting for confirmation, but if I had to bet… my money's on Marta Von Hohenfels."

Callum folded his arms, his brow furrowed as he studied the board. "If it is Marta Von Hohenfels," he said, his tone laced with confusion, "then I'm completely lost. Why would Müller be carrying a pornographic dvd, one that just happens to star Eckhart and Hohenfels?" He turned to Adrian, eyes sharp, as if expecting a simple, logical answer to something that was anything but.

Adrian met his gaze, then shifted his attention to the rest of the team. His voice was measured but firm. "We have four names on this board," he said, gesturing to each in turn. "And as of today, we have three corresponding photographs. We can already establish a connection, one that ties them together through a single piece of evidence: this dvd.

"Two of the names star in it. One of the names was caught carrying it. That alone tells us something. But the real question is, where does Mr. Big fit into all of this?"

At that, Adrian turned and pointed to the last name on the board: Clarkson.

A heavy silence settled over the room as the implications sank in. If Clarkson, the elusive figure they had been trying to pin down, was connected to this, then they were dealing with something far more complex than they had anticipated.

Mathew had seemed lost in thought, his gaze unfocused as if he were miles away. Then, suddenly, his eyes snapped to Adrian, and he barked, "What the hell is Müller doing in London? And when did he arrive?"

Adrian, leaning against the table with arms crossed, remained unfazed. "Well, I don't know why he's here or when exactly he arrived," he said casually. "But I do know that he drove here, all the way from St. Moritz."

A heavy silence fell over the room, broken only by the rhythmic ticking of the large Thomas Kent railway clock in the corridor outside.

Mathew blinked, trying to process it. "Drove… in a… car?" His words came slowly as the implications sank in. Then, his voice sharpened. "Where the hell is his car?"

Adrian raised an eyebrow, as if surprised by the question. "Far as I know, it should still be at Finsbury Park Station, same as Müller. He's being held there until his court appearance this morning."

Mathew spun toward Nicole, his voice crisp and authoritative. "Find that car, Sergeant! Have it brought here immediately and get Forensics onto it. I want every inch of it examined, fingerprints, drugs, surveillance footage, everything."

Nicole gave a sharp nod, already reaching for her phone.

"And," Mathew continued, his mind now racing ahead, "get someone to intercept Müller's hearing. I don't care what you charge him with, beef up the charges with anything that'll stick. We can't risk him walking out of there."

Nicole was already in motion, her voice brisk as she spoke into her phone.

Adrian exchanged a glance with Callum, then back at Mathew. "You think there's something in that car?"

Mathew's jaw tightened in a grin as his Aussie accent momentarily surfaced. "I reckon there just might be, mate!."

Nicole called across the room to Mathew, who was standing at his desk with Callum. "It's all happening," she reported. "We should hear back from the prosecutor at Finsbury Court in about an hour, and forensics will update us once they get Müller's car in later today."

Mathew nodded, processing the information, but before he could respond, Nicole continued, her tone shifting to something lighter. "In the meantime," she said, glancing around the room, "how about we head down to the canteen and grab some morning tea while we can?"

For a moment, there was silence. Then, as if on cue, Callum smirked, and Adrian let out a short chuckle. It was almost amusing how casually she had said it, forgetting, as everyone in the office so often did, that Mathew wasn't just one of them, he was a Prince. A future king. And yet, here they were, treating him like any other colleague, suggesting a quick break over tea and biscuits.

Mathew, however, didn't seem to mind. In fact, he welcomed it. He glanced at Callum, then Adrian, before turning back to Nicole with a slight grin. "Sounds like a plan, Sergeant," he said.

And with that, the team filed out of the office, seizing the rare opportunity for a moment of normalcy before the chaos resumed.

An Invitation from the King

"No fucking way."

Mathew stood frozen in the foyer, staring at the letter he had just pulled from the holder. The embossed royal seal gleamed under the light, the heavy parchment unmistakable. It was from the King.

They had only just returned from a productive day at Scotland Yard. Callum had been quick to organise drinks at the bar, and Mathew, on his way through, had absently opened what he assumed was just another formal correspondence, until he saw the contents.

Callum, already nursing his drink, caught Mathew's expression. He smirked. "What is it, old chap?" he called across the room in that exaggerated Downton Abbey tone they often used to tease each other. "Don't let your drink get warm!"

Mathew exhaled sharply, still staring at the letter. "It's an invitation," he muttered, shaking his head, "to go stalking at Balmoral. On Monday." He handed the letter to Callum and reached for his drink. "I'll have to tell them I'm far too busy to attend. I'm not exactly keen on that sort of shit anyway."

Callum's smirk faded. He set his glass down. "I wouldn't do that if I were you, old boy," he said, his voice suddenly serious. "That would really put you at odds with the King. Remember, we agreed we need him as an ally, not an enemy."

Mathew waved him off. "It's only shooting, Callum. It's not important."

Callum arched a brow. "Maybe not to you, but to him? Being in his company, spending time together, this means the world to him. Trust me, refusing would be a massive mistake." He picked up the letter again, scanning the details. His expression darkened. "Shit… You have to be there next Monday. How long has this been sitting up there in the mail rack?"

Mathew exhaled. "It was stuck behind a BRW magazine in the rack. It must have fallen out when I pulled the magazine just now."

He frowned, realising the gravity of the situation. The King had actually asked him weeks ago whether he enjoyed hunting, and at the time, Mathew had confused it with fox hunting. Clearly, this invitation had been planned for a while.

Callum didn't waste another second. "We'll hardly have time to get you properly kitted out and get up there in time," he muttered, already pulling out his phone. "I'll call Walker & Hawkes and see if they can fit us in tomorrow. They don't open on weekends, but maybe, just maybe, they'll make an exception for you."

As he dialled, Mathew took another sip of his drink, staring at the invitation. His father wanted him at Balmoral. A formal, personal request.

Maybe Callum was right. Maybe refusing wasn't an option.

Callum had enthusiastically suggested they take his Aston Martin DB12 for the trip, citing the fact that he hadn't had much of a chance to drive it lately. At the time, it had seemed like a brilliant idea, what better way to arrive at Balmoral than in a sleek, high-performance coupe?

However, by Sunday morning, as they stood in the driveway trying to pack, the reality of their choice became painfully clear.

Stuffing all their gear into the Aston Martin was proving to be a logistical nightmare. The luggage space was minimal, and the two-door coupe was hardly built for hauling hunting equipment. They managed to squeeze in their overnight bags, boots, and weather gear with some creative manoeuvring, but when it came to Callum's rifle, the one he had intended to loan to Mathew, it became immediately obvious that there was simply no way it was going to fit.

Callum sighed, hands on his hips as he surveyed the overstuffed car. "Well, bollocks to that," he muttered. "Unless we strap it to the bloody roof, this isn't happening."

Mathew, leaning against the passenger door with his arms crossed, smirked. "I don't think turning up at Balmoral with a rifle bungee-corded to the car would make the best impression."

Callum rolled his eyes. "Fine. You'll just have to borrow one from Balmoral."

Mathew shrugged. "Works for me."

With that, they finally shut the boot, after what felt like an elaborate game of luggage Tetris, and slid into their seats. As Callum fired up the DB12, the engine growled to life, and despite the morning's packing frustrations, Mathew couldn't help but grin.

Cramped or not, this was going to be one hell of a drive.

It was Callum's first trip to Balmoral, and he had no idea of the exact route. He relied entirely on the car's GPS to guide them, trusting the Aston Martin's navigation to sort out the details. As they roared down the driveway of the residence, he cast a sideways glance at Mathew and smirked.

"So, can you speak Scotts?" he asked, adopting an exaggerated Scottish accent.

Mathew chuckled. "Not a word. But I do a mean Sean Connery impression."

With a laugh, they settled in for what was to be a nine-hour drive, broken up by a planned lunch stop at the Royal Penrith Hotel.

By early afternoon, they pulled into the historic Royal Penrith Hotel, a charming old establishment known for its hearty food and excellent selection of ales. Opting for a classic pub meal, they enjoyed an excellent lunch, each washing it down with a pint of Reliance Pale Ale.

Mathew couldn't help but notice a few curious glances from other patrons. One or two seemed to recognise him, their expressions shifting from casual observation to something more akin to realisation. However, no one approached, and MI5, ever watchful, ensured that they remained undisturbed.

As they finished their drinks, Callum leaned back in his chair, sighing contentedly. "Damn good pint."

Mathew nodded. "Yeah. Almost makes up for spending half the morning folded into that bloody car."

Callum grinned. "Ah, but you love it."

Mathew rolled his eyes, but he couldn't help but smile.

The final stretch of the journey was long and wet, with steady rain drumming against the DB12's windshield as they wound their way through the Scottish Highlands. The rolling green hills and mist-covered peaks would have been breathtaking in clearer weather, but as darkness fell, visibility became increasingly poor.

At 6:30 PM, after what felt like an eternity on the road, they finally arrived at Balmoral Castle.

As they pulled up to the grand entrance, the rain still coming down in sheets, they were met by the Housekeeper, a warm yet professional woman who welcomed them inside and then instructed her staff where our rooms where.

"Welcome to Balmoral your Highness. You're jest in time," she informed them. "There's a wee dinner toneet in honour of all six of the invited shooting guests, plus yee sen and yee laddie. The King will no be arriving til late, so you'll be the heed of the table toneet sir and your fine equerry will be seated to yee left"

Callum, shaking the rain from his coat, raised an eyebrow at Mathew. "Twelve, huh? Looks like this won't just be a quiet little hunting trip."

Mathew exhaled, glancing around the opulent interior of the castle. "No… looks like it won't be, but man…just look at this place…" They easily found the bar after settling into their rooms. The staff in the room had served their choice of drinks to them and they sat at the edge of the half round bar, Mathew had found a guest list in his room in an envelope addressed to him and marked confidential, he had brought it down to the bar and now passed it to Callum, "Anyone you know?" He asked as Callum, looked at the list.

     Max Barrington

His Royal Highness, Prince Mathew.

Callum Gibb

Duke Alistair Montrose

Earl Sebastian Pembroke

Brigadier James Stirling

Sir Edmund Fairfax

Lord Henry Ashford

Count Wilhelm von Hohenfels

As Callum read the list, the heavy oak doors of the drawing room swung open, and three men, seemingly in their sixties, entered with the easy confidence of those well-accustomed to such gatherings. Almost immediately, the ever-attentive staff swooped in, presenting them with drinks before they even had to ask. Their sharp, discerning eyes scanned the room as they conversed quietly amongst themselves. It was clear from their expressions that none of them immediately recognised Mathew or Callum.

As the group moved closer, one of the men, a tall figure with silvered hair and a military bearing, extended his hand towards Callum. "James Stirling," he introduced himself in a clipped, authoritative tone, shaking Callum's hand firmly. The others followed suit, offering their names with the ease of practiced formality.

Just as introductions were concluding, the remaining three guests arrived, stepping into the warmly lit bar for pre-dinner drinks. There was a momentary lull in conversation as fresh rounds of drinks were served, and Callum took the opportunity to introduce Mathew, exactly as they had agreed upon beforehand.

"This is Mathew Wynasleigh," Callum said smoothly, his tone deliberately casual.

However, the reaction from the guests was immediate. A flicker of recognition passed through the group, subtle but unmistakable. The name alone had been enough. Despite Callum's attempt at discretion, they all instinctively deferred to Mathew, dipping their heads in respect.

"Your Highness," one of them murmured with a knowing smile, and the others followed suit, acknowledging him with the reverence due to his title.

Mathew sighed inwardly but accepted their courtesies with a small nod. So much for keeping a low profile. Mathew had noticed a name on the list that he had intended to draw to Callum's attention but he hadn't had the time with the other guests arriving and now it looked like he would have to wait until after dinner.

As each person sat at the table they observed the carefully prepared menu conveying the theme of the hunt.

The menu for the hunting party's first night's dinner at Balmoral was a carefully curated selection of fine British cuisine, emphasising seasonal Scottish ingredients and traditional royal estate fare. The dining table, set in the grand hall with flickering candlelight reflecting off the polished silverware, featured the following courses:

First Course

Scottish Cullen Skink – A rich and creamy smoked haddock soup with leeks, potatoes, and a hint of parsley, served with freshly baked oatcakes.

Second Course

Venison Carpaccio – Thinly sliced wild venison from the Balmoral estate, dressed with juniper-infused olive oil, shaved parmesan, and foraged microgreens.

Main Course

Roast Saddle of Highland Venison – Perfectly roasted venison, served with buttered neeps and tatties, braised red cabbage, and a redcurrant and whisky jus.

Loch Fyne Salmon en Croûte – Delicate Scottish salmon fillet wrapped in golden puff pastry with a lemon and dill cream sauce, served with wild asparagus and baby carrots.

Side Dishes

Dauphinoise Potatoes – Thinly sliced potatoes layered with cream, garlic, and nutmeg, baked to a golden crisp.
Steamed Seasonal Greens – A selection of fresh greens, including kale, sprouting broccoli, and sugar snap peas.

Dessert

Cranachan – A classic Scottish dessert of whipped cream, toasted oats, raspberries, and a drizzle of heather honey, finished with a splash of single malt whisky.

Cheese Course

Scottish Artisan Cheese Selection – A variety of Scotland's finest cheeses, including Isle of Mull Cheddar, Strathdon Blue, and Clava Brie, served with quince jelly, oatcakes, and walnuts.

After Dinner

Freshly Brewed Highland Coffee & Petit Fours – Handmade chocolates, shortbread, and whisky truffles.

Accompanying the meal was an expertly chosen selection of wines, including a deep-bodied Bordeaux for the venison and a crisp Chablis for the salmon, along with a post-dinner offering of fine Scottish single malt whisky, ensuring a warm and convivial close to the evening. As Mathew savoured the last bite of his Cranachan, he couldn't help but wonder if the King truly understood what he was missing out on. The meal had been nothing short of spectacular, yet the sheer richness of the cuisine made him question whether he could endure an entire week of such indulgence. He had always enjoyed fine food, but there was something almost overwhelming about course after course of meticulously prepared Scottish fare, each more decadent than the last. A simpler meal wouldn't go astray, he mused.

Throughout dinner, the conversation remained polite, with only the occasional mention of the day's travel and the anticipation of the hunt. The only toasts made were the customary ones, first, "To The King!" which was raised with a deep reverence, and then, "To the

King's Heir!" a moment that had drawn subtle glances toward Mathew, though he chose to acknowledge them with nothing more than a small, appreciative nod.

It wasn't long before most of the guests retired for the evening, the heavy meal and travel fatigue catching up with them. However, a few lingered in the lounge, where the staff had laid out an exceptional Berry Bros. & Rudd old tawny port, the deep amber liquid gleaming in the firelight. The scent of oak, dried fruit, and warm spice filled the air as crystal glasses clinked softly against one another.

Mathew, opting to enjoy a glass himself, had positioned himself comfortably in one of the deep leather armchairs when he realised he was now seated across from the very person he had wanted to draw Callum's attention to on the guest list. Count Wilhelm von Hohenfels carried himself with the effortless grace of old-world aristocracy, an impeccably dressed man in his late sixties, his neatly combed silver hair, piercing blue eyes, and perfectly tailored dinner jacket spoke of a life steeped in privilege and refinement. He held his glass of port with deliberate elegance, swirling the deep amber liquid as though contemplating its very essence. His gaze, keen and discerning, settled on Mathew with an expression that suggested their conversation had been inevitable.

Mathew took a slow sip of his drink, meeting the Count's eyes. This, he thought, was about to become a far more interesting evening than he had anticipated.

"The name Von Hohenfels, Count..." Mathew began, his tone casual but his intent anything but.

"Please," Wilhelm interjected smoothly, a faint smile touching his lips, "call me Wilhelm. Or Will, as my friends do, Your Highness."

Mathew inclined his head slightly. "Thank you, Will. I was just wondering about the name Von Hohenfels, it's rather distinctive. Would you, by any chance, know of a Marta Von Hohenfels? She worked with the avalanche monitoring control at Corvatsch."

At the mention of the name, Wilhelm straightened abruptly. The change in his demeanour was subtle, but telling. His fingers tightened around the stem of his glass, his lips pressing together for the briefest moment before he exhaled.

"Oh… you knew Marta?" His voice, though composed, carried a note of solemnity. "Such a tragedy… yar." He lowered his head slightly, as if in silent tribute.

Mathew's pulse quickened. He hadn't expected that reaction. "What… has something happened to her?" His grip on his glass tightened as he leaned in slightly, eyes locked onto Wilhelm's. "I wasn't aware."

Wilhelm gave a slow nod, swirling his port once more before taking a measured sip. "She was killed in an accident in München… just last week. I was at her funeral." His voice was steady, but there was an unmistakable weight behind his words. "She was my brother's eldest daughter." A pause. "Very sad."

Mathew blinked. This was not what he had expected. He had come seeking information, perhaps a clue, a connection, but instead, he found himself facing something far more immediate. Marta was dead.

Wilhelm refilled his glass and studied Mathew with quiet scrutiny. "How well did you know her?" He leaned in slightly, his blue eyes narrowing in interest.

Mathew hesitated. He couldn't possibly tell this man, the grieving uncle, that his niece might have been involved in the tragic avalanche. Worse still, that she may have starred in a pornographic film. Instead, he chose his words carefully.

"Just through a colleague, and only briefly, it was the unusual name I suppose. What happened?" Mathew asked cautiously. "That is… if you don't mind discussing it."

Wilhelm let out a slow breath and shook his head. "No… no. It's fine." He took another sip before continuing, his voice quieter now. "She fell off the platform at Heimeranplatz train station. They say it was an accident. The security footage doesn't show much... just her standing near the edge, then suddenly... gone."

Mathew swallowed. "Nothing unusual? No one near her?"

Wilhelm shook his head. "Nothing definitive. Just... one of those horrible things, I suppose."

Mathew wasn't sure he believed that.

And judging by the shadow in Wilhelm's eyes, neither did he. A quick glance at Callum confirmed Mathew's suspicion, his friend had been listening to the conversation just as intently. Callum's subtle eye roll spoke volumes, a silent acknowledgment of the unspoken thoughts they both shared. It was a familiar gesture between them, one that conveyed amusement, skepticism, and intrigue all at once.

Mathew turned his attention back to the count, now feeling a shift in his perception of the hunting trip. What had initially seemed like an unnecessary royal obligation, an antiquated tradition he could have done without, was now proving to be something far more valuable.

Perhaps this week at Balmoral wouldn't be a complete waste of time after all. If anything, it had already presented an unexpected opportunity, and Mathew had learned long ago that such opportunities were rarely accidental.

Leaning back in his chair, he swirled the last of his port in its crystal glass and allowed a small, knowing smile to form at the corner of his lips. Yes, he thought. I'm quite glad I decided to come.

The King was already seated at the breakfast table when Mathew arrived, looking remarkably fresh despite having arrived at some ungodly hour during the night. He was in high spirits, eager to get the hunting underway, and wasted no time in discussing the day's plans with the assembled guests.

On the long oak breakfast table, alongside the silver coffee pots and platters of smoked salmon and scrambled eggs, lay the neatly printed hunting lists. The party had been divided into three groups, each consisting of three shooters plus a bearer to assist them. Mathew barely glanced at the assignments, he just wanted the day to be over. This entire event felt foreign to him, an outdated tradition that held little appeal.

The King himself was among the nine shooters, and the plan was straightforward. One group would hunt deer, another would pursue hares, and the last would take on wood pigeons. Each group would remain together for the week, rotating through the different game every second day.

The final day of hunting, Friday, would culminate in a grand gala dinner at the castle, where the hunters' wives and partners would join them for the evening. Afterward, the guests would begin departing Balmoral over the weekend, returning to their respective homes.

Mathew sighed, stirring his coffee absentmindedly. A long week stretched ahead, filled with activities that meant little to him. Yet, after last night's conversation, he couldn't shake the feeling that this trip might hold more significance than he had first thought.

Aldrich Müller

Back in their office at Scotland Yard bright and early on Monday morning, Mathew and Callum were greeted with an update from Sergeant Evans. She wasted no time diving into the latest developments.

"Müller has been sentenced to six months on drug charges," she announced, leaning against Mathew's desk with a satisfied grin. "It should be enough to hold him while the CIB builds a case for the other charges they want to nail him with."

Mathew, who had barely settled into his chair, frowned at the mention of 'other charges.' He shot a questioning look at Nicole, who was clearly waiting for his reaction.

"What other charges? The CIB? What am I missing here, Nicole?" he asked, intrigued.

Lowering her voice slightly, but still loud enough for Callum to hear, she leaned in. "It's a bit hush-hush for now… but it's about the murder of Blair Washington."

Mathew sat upright, his attention fully locked on her. "What?" His voice was sharp with surprise.

"They found a gun in Müller's car," Nicole continued, her tone almost casual, but her eyes flickered with significance.

Mathew's stunned expression said it all. "What?! You're telling me Müller is connected to Washington's murder? Are ballistics confirming the link?"

Nicole nodded. "That's exactly what we're waiting on. Forensics are running the tests now. If the gun matches, Müller won't just be looking at a few months in prison, he'll be going away for a long time."

Mathew exhaled, running a hand through his hair as he exchanged a glance with Callum. "This just got interesting. Tell me everything you know, Nicole."

Sergeant Nicole Evans handed over the verbal report to Senior Constable Julie Coogan, who had been closely monitoring Müller's case. Julie adjusted her glasses, flipped open her notebook, and began reading aloud in a measured tone.

"A detailed search of Müller's vehicle, a 2024 BMW M60, uncovered various drugs in different quantities," she reported. "His clothing was scattered across the back seat and packed into the rear compartment, suggesting he was preparing for his return to St. Moritz. Alongside his personal belongings, officers found two cartons of bottled water and four sealed bottles of duty-free Johnnie Walker Black Label Scotch whisky."

She paused, letting the information settle before continuing.

"An Apple paper bag was also discovered on the front passenger seat. Inside, officers found the empty packaging of an Apple Ultra 2 watch and a set of Apple AirPods Pro 2. A card was tucked inside the bag, bearing a handwritten note in blue biro that read: 'A little something to help on the long drive home. M.'"

Julie glanced up. "There was no name, no signature."

Mathew frowned. "And the watch and AirPods?"

"They were found on Müller's person," Julie confirmed. "Presumably taken straight from those boxes."

She took a breath before moving on to the most significant discovery.

"And then we found the weapon," she said, her voice steady. "A Glock G42 compact .380 auto. This particular model is built from polycarbonate, making it incredibly lightweight. It's just 25mm, one inch, thick and 151mm, six inches, long, with a loaded weight of 450 grams, or about sixteen ounces."

Mathew and Callum exchanged a look, both recognising the implications of such a small, easily concealed firearm.

Julie continued. "It was found taped to the inside of the spare wheel rim, hidden within the inflated tyre itself. Whoever placed it there knew exactly what they were doing."

A heavy silence settled over the room. Mathew exhaled sharply. "Alright," he said, his mind already working through the possibilities. "Now we just need to find out if that gun is linked to Washington's murder."

Julie nodded. "Just waiting on forensics."

"Good," Mathew said, his jaw tightening. "Let's make sure we get answers, fast."

Mathew then went to the whiteboard and put a red circle around the name of Marta Von Hohenfels and announced to his crew that she was dead and added a brief outline of the circumstances finishing with…. "And then there were three!"

Later that afternoon Mathew received a call whilst he was still in the Scotland Yard office, from Chief Superintendent Neville Fleming, asking if His Highness could find a few minutes to call into his office. Asking Sergeant Evans directions to the Chief Superintendent's office and taking Callum with him Mathew set off with an open mind.

The view from Fleming's office was nothing short of spectacular, an uninterrupted panorama of London's skyline stretching out beneath a crisp blue sky. The afternoon sun reflected off the glass facades of the city's high-rises, casting shifting patterns of light across the room. The scene was a stark contrast to the gravity of the conversation that was about to unfold.

Fleming, leaning back in his chair, seemed to be in a much better mood than the last time Mathew had spoken to him. Or perhaps, Mathew thought, he was simply in a clearer frame of mind, having had time to process the latest developments. Regardless, there was no mistaking the bluntness in his tone as he got straight to the point.

"The ballistics report is in," Fleming stated flatly. "No doubt about it. The gun we found in Müller's car is the same one that fired the .380 projectile lodged in Blair Washington's skull."

The words sent an involuntary shiver down Mathew's spine. He exhaled slowly, absorbing the confirmation. It wasn't just suspicion anymore, it was fact.

Fleming continued, his tone edged with reluctant admiration. "Pretty smart hidey hole he had for the weapon, sir. Taping it inside the rim of the spare wheel, tucked away in the inflation cavity? Ingenious. And given that the weapon's polycarbonate frame wouldn't trigger standard x-ray alarms, it's likely that it would have sailed straight past Border Force at the LeShuttle checkpoint. Same trick might've been used to smuggle it into the country in the first place."

Mathew nodded, his mind already racing ahead.

Fleming pushed on, his fingers drumming lightly on the case file in front of him. "There were no serial numbers, completely ground off. Forensics will run it through the special x-ray to recover them, though I'm not sure what good it'll do us at this stage." He paused, then leaned forward slightly, lowering his voice.

"But sir," he said, a new weight in his tone, "where do we go from here? And I don't mean with the murder case. I mean the other issue, the one you and MI5 have been chasing."

Mathew met Fleming's gaze, instantly understanding the subtext of his question. The murder of Blair Washington was a significant breakthrough, but it was merely one thread in a much larger and more intricate web, one that extended far beyond a single crime scene.

Leaning forward slightly, Mathew's tone shifted, a mix of curiosity and familiarity creeping in. "Neville," he said, glancing toward the polished wooden bureau against the wall. "Those bottles of Dimple Haig sitting up there, are they the real deal, or just for show?"

Fleming followed his gaze, a flicker of amusement crossing his face before he responded. "His Highness should know I don't deal in counterfeits," he said with a smirk. Rising from his chair, he strode over to the cabinet beneath the bottles, retrieving three short

                                          Max Barrington

glasses. With practiced ease, he lifted one of the bottles, breaking the seal with a quiet pop before pouring three generous measures of the rich amber liquid.

Returning to the desk, he slid a glass each toward Mathew and Callum, then raised his own in a rare moment of camaraderie. His previously clipped, professional tone softened ever so slightly as he offered a simple but sincere toast.

"Good health, gentlemen," he said, holding his glass aloft.

Mathew took his glass, feeling the reassuring weight of the cut crystal tumbler in his palm. The rich amber liquid within caught the light, casting warm, golden hues across the polished surface of Fleming's desk. As he lifted it to his lips, the aroma of finely aged whisky filled his senses, smoky and smooth, with the faintest undertone of spice. It was a drink meant for savouring, but Mathew barely registered its complexity. His mind was already turning over the implications of what he was about to say.

Clinking glasses with the others, he met Callum's gaze briefly before taking a measured sip. The warmth of the whisky spread through him, but he knew all too well that whatever lay ahead in this tangled affair would require far more than good health to navigate.

Setting his glass down, he leaned forward slightly, his voice lower now, more deliberate. He brought Fleming up to speed with the latest developments, everything they knew about the avalanche, from the initial reports to the grim confirmation of Marta Von Hohenfels' death. Whether it had been an accident or something more sinister, he couldn't yet say. But if he were a betting man, he would wager that the same person they now had locked up downstairs, Müller, had played a part in it. How, exactly, was still unclear, but the likelihood of his involvement was too high to dismiss.

Fleming listened intently, his fingers idly turning the base of his glass against the desk. When Mathew finished, a silence settled between them, thick with unspoken possibilities.

Mathew exhaled, tapping a finger against the side of his tumbler as a thought took shape. "I wonder," he mused aloud, "if we could trace Müller's route. Find out where he stopped on his way here." He glanced toward Fleming. "Would it be possible to pull records, hotel bookings, fuel stops, anything that could give us a lead?"

Then, as though the idea had struck him mid-sentence, he added, "I wonder if it could have been Heimeranplatz?"

Fleming's expression remained unreadable, but there was a shift in his posture, an almost imperceptible tightening of the jaw, a narrowing of the eyes.

"Heimeranplatz," Mathew repeated slowly, letting the name settle between them. "Now, that would be interesting."

Fleming frowned, his brows knitting together. "Heimeranplatz? Where the fuck is Heimeranplatz?"

Mathew merely raised his hands in a gesture of patience, watching as Fleming strode across the room to his map cabinet. He flipped through several folders before selecting a large map of Germany, spreading it out on a nearby table. His finger traced along the familiar cities, Munich, Berlin, Hamburg, before finally landing on the marked location.

A moment of silence stretched between them as Fleming studied it, his sharp mind already calculating possible connections.

It was quickly agreed that MI6 would take the lead in retracing Müller's route into Britain. Every stop he made, every possible contact, every piece of surveillance they could access, nothing would be overlooked. If Heimeranplatz held any significance, they would uncover it.

At the same time, they turned their attention to Müller himself. A plea bargain was now firmly on the table. If he cooperated, if he provided useful intelligence on the Corvatsch avalanche, it could open the door to an even bigger revelation, Clarkson's potential involvement. If Müller could tie Clarkson not only to the avalanche but also to the murder of Blair Washington, then they had real leverage.

The deal was clear: silence would mean a life sentence. Co-operation, however, could reduce it, perhaps to fifteen years, maybe even less. The choice was Müller's to make.

Mathew had a feeling that, when faced with the cold reality of a lifetime behind bars, Müller would start talking.

Aldrich Müller had been sentenced to six months at HMP Wormwood Scrubs, a grim and imposing facility nestled near Kensington. It was a far cry from the luxury he had once enjoyed, but he had little choice other than to endure it.

Early that morning, before breakfast, a duty prison officer stopped by his cell with a word of warning. "Police are coming to see you after breakfast," the officer said flatly. "Don't dally."

Müller had barely reacted. He had expected as much.

Later, as he stood in the breakfast line, tray in hand, another inmate behind him would recall hearing a sharp, deafening explosion, an instant before blood sprayed from both sides of Müller's head. The man, a former soldier who had served in Afghanistan, recognised the unmistakable effect of a high-velocity headshot.

Panic spread through the canteen as prisoners and staff instinctively ducked for cover. The air was thick with the metallic scent of blood, the stunned silence punctuated by shouts and the clatter of trays hitting the floor. Müller's lifeless body crumpled onto the steel surface beneath him, motionless, his breakfast forgotten.

Within moments, the prison was placed on full lockdown. Armed response teams were mobilised, but it took forty-five tense minutes before the 'all clear' was given. Müller's body was eventually removed to the prison hospital for a preliminary examination before being transferred to the forensic sciences unit for a full autopsy.

The initial examination revealed two small, precise entry wounds on either side of his skull, where his ears had once been. His eardrums were obliterated, leaving behind only scorched, torn flesh.

Forensic technicians conducted an exhaustive sweep of the canteen and its surrounding areas, but no traditional bullet casings or projectiles were found. Instead, they uncovered microscopic fragments of various materials, including human bone and tissue, along with remnants of thermoplastic polymer and acrylonitrile butadiene.

But it was the final discovery that sent a chill through the forensic team: traces of cyclotrimethylenetrinitramine, better known as RDX (Royal Demolition Explosive).

Müller hadn't been shot in the conventional sense. He had been executed with surgical precision, by an explosive device concealed within, or on, his own body.

It was later revealed that Müller was rarely seen without his ear pods in place, a constant fixture in his daily routine. The small white devices were practically an extension of him, often playing music or taking calls, depending on his mood. But on that fateful morning, no one could say for certain whether he had been wearing them when the explosion occurred.

In an attempt to gather more details, investigators searched his cell meticulously. Among the various personal items and clutter that filled the small, prison-standard room, the charging case for his ear pods was found, but it was completely empty. The ear pods themselves were missing, and it was presumed that Müller had been wearing them at the time of his death. This raised the unsettling possibility that they could have been the key to the explosion. Forensics, however, would take another two months of painstaking investigation to uncover the full extent of the truth.

After an extensive examination, the forensic team confirmed their suspicions: Müller's ear pods had indeed been tampered with. Hidden inside the small, inconspicuous devices was an explosive charge, likely triggered by a signal from a mobile telephone. It seemed that whoever had orchestrated Müller's death had gone to great lengths to make it appear as a freak accident, embedding the lethal device in something so ordinary and unassuming as a pair of ear pods.

The revelation sent shockwaves through the investigation. The sophistication of the plot raised more questions than answers. How had the signal been sent? Who had sent it? And, perhaps most chilling of all, how had Müller been targeted in such a precise and methodical manner? HRH Prince Mathew was pretty sure he knew the answer to that question.

Bruno Eckhart

Bruno was no novice when it came to electronics. With his homemade scanner in hand, he swiftly disabled the surveillance cameras, bypassed the burglar alarm, and effortlessly unlocked the electronic door lock. The ease with which he breached the system astounded him, it was laughable that a shop specializing in sporting goods, particularly firearms, would have such a poorly designed security setup.

Now standing before the rifle rack, he surveyed the selection with a calculated gaze. A sleek, black stainless steel chain, light gauge but highly polished, ran through the trigger guards of the rifles, eyeing the chain with mild curiosity. With a firm tug, the links clattered against the metal, sliding easily through the trigger guards.

Bruno had already set his sights on the weapon he wanted. He had visited the store days earlier, feigning interest as a customer, carefully noting the inventory. The rifle he had chosen was exactly what he needed, precision, power, and reliability. But Britain's strict firearm regulations had made legal acquisition impossible for someone like him, a visitor with no gun license and no legal avenue to obtain one.

None of that mattered now. The rifle was within reach. It was a Purdey bolt-action 6.5 Creedmoor, a masterpiece of craftsmanship and precision, equipped with a Swarovski Z8i 13.3x42 scope, one of the finest optics money could buy. This rifle was built for accuracy, capable of delivering lethal precision at long distances. Bruno admired it for a moment, running his fingers along the sleek barrel, before shifting his focus to the more pressing issue, finding the right ammunition.

That turned out to be the most time-consuming part of the night. The ammunition wasn't stored in plain sight, which meant he had to search for it. Grabbing a razor-sharp hunting knife from the counter display, he went to work, prying open nearly every drawer beneath the rifle rack. The locks were flimsy, cheap, and no match for his determination. Wood splintered, metal hinges creaked in protest, and drawer after drawer was rifled through until, finally, he found what he was looking for. A full box of 6.5mm cartridges.

Bruno wasted no time. He selected a genuine leather rifle case from the display, its rich brown hide stitched to perfection, and carefully placed the rifle and ammunition inside. With the case slung over his shoulder, he stepped through the front door of the shop and into the cool night air.

The street was silent, the only sound his own measured footsteps as he made his way back to his rented flat, just one hundred and seventy meters away. He walked calmly, deliberately, as though he had simply purchased the rifle rather than stolen it. There were no alarms, no police sirens, no shouts of alarm. By the time anyone discovered the break-in, Bruno would be long gone, the Purdey and its deadly potential now in his possession.

Bruno had purchased a second-hand Range Rover Vogue, an older model, but in excellent condition. More importantly, it was affordable, which was a crucial factor for him. He had roughly Fr80,000 left from the Fr100,000 that Marta had given him. She had insisted that it was all she had, swearing up and down that there was nothing more. Bruno, of course, had played his part well, acting as if he might accept her word, until he made it clear that if she didn't pay up, he would take the video straight to her father, Heinrich Von Hohenfels.

In truth, he didn't even have a copy of the damned video. But Marta didn't know that.

"Heimeranplatz Station," he had told her coldly. "Get the cash and meet me there."

The gullible, desperate fool had fallen for it.

She had shown up just as instructed, clutching the money, pleading with him not to leave. She had grabbed onto his jacket lapel, her grip tight, her face filled with desperation. He had tried to shake her off, but she wouldn't let go. The station was crowded, people moving in all directions, bumping into them. And then, suddenly, she was gone.

One moment she had been holding onto him, the next, she was screaming.

Bruno had turned just in time to see her fall.

And he had kept walking.

No hesitation. No second glance.

As if he had no idea who she was. As if he had no idea what had just happened. He hadn't wanted to hurt her, he though he had loved her at one time, but she had….how could she have done to him what she had done?

His rented flat on the first floor had a clear view across the street into 74 Whitehall Road, Harrow, the residence of Melvin Clarkson. It hadn't been difficult to track him down. Technically, it was just a flat, not a home. Bruno doubted Clarkson actually lived there; it seemed more like a convenient hideaway, a place where he could bring the young men he picked up on the streets of London.

At first, something had puzzled Bruno, Clarkson always arrived in a taxi. But oddly enough, the taxi never left right away. It would remain parked overnight, only to depart again in the morning. That didn't make sense, unless, of course, Clarkson wasn't a passenger at all.

Then, it clicked.

Clarkson owned the taxi.

The bastard had been using an old London cab as his personal cover, blending seamlessly into the city's landscape. No one ever looked twice at a black cab driving around London. It was brilliant. Disgustingly brilliant.

And now, that same taxi was parked beside the small block of flats, while Bruno's Range Rover was stationed a block away, out of sight. He watched as Clarkson emerged from the building, casually making his way toward the vehicle.

Bruno inhaled deeply, settling the crosshairs of his scope just below Clarkson's head. The distance was roughly forty meters, and he had zeroed the rifle at seventy-five. A slight compensation was necessary, but nothing he couldn't manage.

He exhaled.

Squeezed the trigger.

Clarkson dropped instantly, collapsing like a puppet with its strings cut. The 95-grain soft-point projectile had done its job, piercing through the centre of his skull and violently ejecting his brain matter from the back of his head. The shot had been clean, precise. Lethal.

Bruno didn't need to check. He knew Clarkson was dead.

Without hesitation, he let the rifle drop to the floor, slipped out of his flat, and hurried down to his waiting Range Rover. He drove the short block to the scene, screeched to a halt, and jumped out with a blanket in hand.

Feigning panic, he rushed toward the fallen man, calling for help, playing the part of a concerned bystander who had just stumbled upon a tragedy. Once the unnecessary help had arrived, concerned pedestrians, a panicked passerby, and soon after, the wail of approaching sirens, Bruno had slipped away unnoticed.

Blending seamlessly into the chaos, he moved with purpose but without haste, disappearing into the labyrinth of side streets and alleyways. By the time the first responders reached Clarkson's lifeless body, Bruno was already miles away, his Range Rover merging effortlessly into the steady flow of London traffic en route to St Moritz via LeShuttle.

The news of Clarkson's mysterious death had filtered to Mathew's group; this was getting ridiculous. They had now lost three of the names on the whiteboard, one by one, crossed out in red. Now, only a single name remained.

Bruno Eckhart.

They had returned to the residence and in the comfort of the bar lounge were analysing the situation of their investigation into the possibility that Prince Arnold may have been implicated somehow, possibly through a connection with Melvin Clarkson.

The first devastating blow to their investigation had been the discovery of Marta von Hohenfels' death. The news had struck like a hammer, sudden, unexpected, and leaving behind more questions than answers.

They had no concrete evidence linking her to the avalanche disaster, yet there were too many coincidences to ignore. What they did know was that she had some connection to Eckart, but the nature of that connection remained a mystery. Was she merely an acquaintance? A pawn in something larger? Or had she been deeply entangled in whatever forces were at play?

Then there was the other suspicion, one they had yet to confirm or disprove. They couldn't shake the uneasy possibility that Marta was the woman in the pornographic film they had uncovered. The resemblance, though not definitive, was enough to raise concerns. If it was her, what did that mean? And if it wasn't, why had her name surfaced in places it had no business being?

Their strongest source of information had been Müller. They had placed high confidence in the plea bargain, believing it would yield most, if not all, of the intelligence they needed. But fate, it seemed, had other plans.

Clarkson, ever the meticulous planner, had prepared for this exact scenario. At some point, he had given Müller a pair of ear pods, loaded with an explosive charge, rigged to detonate upon receiving

     Max Barrington

a signal. A final insurance policy. If Müller were ever caught, he would never have the chance to talk.

And now, Müller was gone.

The loss was a frustrating setback for the investigation, but there was at least one man who wasn't particularly troubled by it, Chief Superintendent Neville Fleming. To him, Müller's death was nothing more than a convenient conclusion. No lengthy trial, no legal wrangling. The gun found in Müller's car had already sealed his fate. Guilty. Case closed.

"Dishes done. Gone and finished," Fleming had muttered under his breath, barely concealing his satisfaction.

And now, the latest to slip from their grasp was Clarkson. His death meant they would most likely never uncover the full extent of his involvement, if any, in orchestrating the avalanche. If he had been responsible, the crucial question remained: why? Had it been a ruthless attempt to clear the way for Prince Arnold to ascend the throne? Or was there another, more insidious motive lurking beneath the surface?

With Clarkson gone, only one name remained on their list, Bruno Eckhart. The last survivor. If he was still alive.

The entire situation had become a tangled web of uncertainty, loose ends, and unanswered questions. But in the end, they had to acknowledge that the result was, in many ways, the same. One by one, those responsible had met their fate. Justice, however unorthodox, had been served.

Callum, ever the cynic, leaned back in his chair, swirling the ice in his glass with an amused smirk. "So much for your Dick Tracy act, old chap. At this rate, you won't have any suspects left to chase! I do hope dear Bruno is safe and well, or you'll be completely out of a job, haha! Pip, pip… hey, what!" He chuckled as he deftly outmanoeuvred the steward for the next round of drinks at the residence bar.

Mathew exhaled slowly, shaking his head in mock despair. "It's quite obvious, old boy," he declared, lifting his glass with exaggerated solemnity. He took a sip, nearly missing his mouth in his enthusiasm, before continuing, "They were all so terrified of me that they committed hara-kiri!"

Callum snorted into his drink as they both burst out laughing as Mathew's 'group' mobile telephone rang. It was Adrian on the line, wanting to know where they were. He had been working on a scenario, one he felt was worth their consideration.

Mathew, however, had already made peace with the fact that the case, while perhaps not solved in the traditional sense, was closed. There was no one left to pursue, no more loose ends that could be tied up with certainty. And yet, for reasons he couldn't quite explain, something in Adrian's voice made him pause. Why not? he thought. There was no harm in hearing him out.

"All right," Mathew said finally. "Come over to the residence."

Callum, who had been listening in, gave a knowing shake of his head before interjecting. "No chance, old boy. Given the security involved, we'll have to send a car for him." He took the phone from Mathew and spoke into it. "We'll have a car collect you, say three o'clock at the main Scotland Yard entrance? Sound good…"Oh, on second thought… Adrian, are you still there?"

There was a brief pause before Adrian's voice came through the line. "Yes, I'm still here."

"Bring the ladies with you," Mathew said. "I'm sure they'd be interested in hearing your prognosis of what may have been."

Callum grinned, clearly pleased with the suggestion. "Good idea, old chap," he said, clapping Mathew on the back.

Mathew reached into his pocket and pulled out his second mobile, the one he had been given at Melbourne Airport before meeting Callum. Stored in it was a number few people had direct access to. He pressed the call button and lifted the phone to his ear.

"Yes, Mathew?" The King's voice was calm but expectant.

"You've probably heard by now that all my suspects have inconveniently dropped off the edge. If you can spare an hour or so this afternoon at the residence bar, one of my colleagues is presenting his scenario on the whole case. Thought you might find it interesting."

There was a brief silence on the line, then the King responded. "Really?… Excellent. See you shortly."

Mathew slipped the phone back into his pocket, turning to Callum with a smirk. "Might be quite the party, old boy, the boss is coming too."

Adrian's Scenario

The six of them were seated around a long, elegantly set table, designed to accommodate ten. Mathew had given precise instructions to the steward, ensuring that the arrangement was both formal and practical. At the head of the table, a place was set for the King, while the opposite end was reserved for himself, the Prince. On one side, a single seat was prepared for the speaker, Adrian, granting him the focus of the room. Across from him, four places were arranged, allowing for Callum, and the three lady police officers to observe and engage in the discussion without obstruction.

It was a well-thought-out setup, Mathew mused as he surveyed the table. The balance of formality and intimacy suited the occasion perfectly. The only thing left was to await the King's arrival.

The King did not keep them waiting. His arrival was so casual, so unassuming, that at first, the two women assumed he was merely another guest joining the gathering. It wasn't until they registered the subtle deference in the room, the barely perceptible shift in posture from those who recognised him, that realisation dawned. Their initial ease gave way to sudden shyness, their conversation faltering as they became acutely aware of his presence.

Sensing their discomfort, the King effortlessly put them at ease. "Hello, all," he said warmly, a hint of amusement in his tone. "Room for one more?"

Without waiting for an answer, he moved gracefully to his designated seat at the head of the table, waving off any attempt to stand in his honour. "Please, stay seated," he insisted with a casual smile as he settled into his chair. His demeanour was relaxed, yet there was an undeniable presence about him, one that commanded both respect and admiration without the need for formality.

Meanwhile, his equerry and MI5 security detail discreetly took their places at a separate table near the entrance, maintaining a watchful but unobtrusive presence.

They waited patiently as the stewards completed their rounds, ensuring that every glass was filled and every need attended to before discreetly withdrawing from the room. Only then did Mathew, still seated, take a moment to introduce each of the police officers who had worked alongside him throughout the case. His introductions were brief but respectful, allowing The King to acknowledge each officer with a nod of appreciation.

With the formalities done, Mathew turned his attention to Adrian. "Whenever you're ready," he said, giving him the floor.

True to his nature, Adrian wasted no time on ceremony. Foregoing any formal address to His Royal Highness, he simply inclined his head in acknowledgment toward The King. There was no defiance in the gesture, nor any intended slight, it was simply the way Adrian's mind worked, shaped by the relentless grip of the disease that had altered the nuances of his social interactions.

If The King was offended, he did not show it. Instead, he leaned back slightly in his chair, his expression one of quiet curiosity as he waited for Adrian to begin. The room, once filled with light conversation and the gentle clinking of glasses, grew still as all eyes turned to the man about to present his theory.

"The avalanche near St. Moritz that killed members of the royal family was, I believe, a deliberate act, orchestrated with the sole purpose of accelerating Prince Arnold's ascension to the throne."

Adrian's voice was firm, his delivery direct. He had no intention of softening the blow or sugarcoating his theory. This was going to be a raw, unfiltered analysis of the events as he saw them, bold, uncompromising, and backed by the weight of his deductions.

The room, which had been filled with a quiet murmur of conversation just moments ago, fell into a heavy silence. All eyes were locked on Adrian, some with intrigue, others with quiet skepticism. The King remained impassive, his expression unreadable, while Mathew and Callum exchanged a subtle glance. They had known Adrian long enough to understand that he was not prone to exaggeration, if he had come to this conclusion, then he had his reasons.

Adrian, unfazed by the intensity of the attention now focused on him, pressed on. "The deaths that followed were not a series of unfortunate coincidences. They were calculated. Executions, if you will. He leaned forward slightly, his eyes scanning the faces before him. "This was not a natural disaster. It was an assassination masked as an act of nature. Sadly, I can't prove it but you will form your own opinion. Maybe like a good book with the last page missing, you will have to use your imagination."

Adrian continued to elaborate on his theory, adding a crucial distinction, one that, if true, could shift the entire perspective on the case.

"It is highly unlikely that Prince Arnold had any knowledge of Clarkson's plan to expedite his rise to the throne," he stated with conviction. "I believe the Prince to be entirely innocent in this matter."

A subtle wave of relief seemed to pass over the room, particularly among those who had worked closely with the royal family. Adrian, however, wasted no time in pressing forward.

"Clarkson, on the other hand," he continued, "was undeniably brilliant, but tragically, his mind operated in the realm of the criminal. He wasn't just a man with means; he was a man who understood how to manipulate circumstances to serve his own objectives."

Adrian's voice took on a measured intensity as he laid out his reasoning. "He selected the King's recreational time with his family as the ideal opportunity for an 'accident.' The very thing that made the trip a moment of leisure, its isolation, its unpredictability, also made it the perfect setting for an assassination disguised as a natural disaster."

He leaned back slightly, giving his words a moment to settle before delivering the next piece of the puzzle.

"But here's the most interesting part. Clarkson wasn't just vaguely aware of avalanche risks, he was deeply invested in them. Recently, he had purchased shares in several ski lodges, treating them as a long-term investment. To protect those investments, he had immersed himself in the study of avalanche behaviour, not just as a precaution, but as a marketing tool, to promote the lodges as 'safe' destinations, well-monitored and secure against natural disasters."

Adrian paused, allowing the weight of his words to sink in. "In the process, he gained knowledge far beyond that of a casual investor. He learned how avalanches form, how they can be predicted, and most importantly, how they can be triggered."

A sharp silence followed. The implications were clear. Clarkson hadn't merely been prepared for an avalanche; he had likely orchestrated one.

"This is where I believe Clarkson may have conceived his plan," Adrian continued, his voice steady and deliberate. "Once he grasped just how unpredictable avalanche monitoring truly was, he would have realised that, unlike many modern security systems, which rely on automated precision and fail-safes, avalanche monitoring remains heavily dependent on human observation and interpretation."

He paused, allowing the weight of his words to settle over the table.

"That single vulnerability, the human factor, was something Clarkson could manipulate. He would have studied the patterns, the variables, the blind spots. He would have known that even the most advanced avalanche warning systems are, at their core, only as reliable as the people operating them."

Adrian leaned forward slightly, his gaze sweeping the room. "And therein lay his opportunity. He didn't need to create some elaborate, foolproof disaster. He simply had to ensure that a natural event happened at precisely the right time, in precisely the right place."

A heavy silence followed. The implications were clear, Clarkson had not only understood the science of avalanches but had also recognised the inherent weaknesses in the monitoring process. He had known exactly how to turn those weaknesses to his advantage.

Adrian took a slow sip of his drink, gathering his thoughts before continuing.

"Clarkson first encountered Müller at one of his ski lodges, where Müller was working as a roustabout and general handyman," he said, setting the stage. "Clarkson's initial impression? Müller wasn't exactly the sharpest tool in the shed, competent enough for menial tasks, but certainly not a mastermind. However, what Müller lacked in intellect, he more than made up for in obedience and loyalty. Clarkson quickly realised that Müller would follow any instruction given to him, without question."

Adrian paused for a moment, letting the words sink in before adding, "At this stage, we should also remember that Clarkson was a homosexual, and we can reasonably assume the same was true for Müller." His eyes swept the table, as if gauging the reaction to this revelation. He leaned forward slightly, lowering his voice just a fraction. "Clarkson would have known that attempting to bribe someone to tamper with scientific instruments, especially in a way that could endanger lives, let alone a royal family, was an impossible proposition. No amount of money could convince a man of integrity to take such a risk." He let the moment hang in the air before adding, "But blackmail? Now, that's a different game entirely."

The implication was clear. Clarkson had not needed to find a willing accomplice, only a vulnerable one.

Adrian leaned back slightly, letting his words settle before continuing.

"Now, here is where I must speculate," he admitted, tapping his fingers lightly on the table. "But based on what we know, I believe Müller's first role in this operation was to observe the staff at the

Corvatsch Avalanche Monitoring Control Centre, looking for a weak link, someone vulnerable. He didn't have to search for long."

. He glanced around the table before pressing on.

"Müller discovered that Eckhart was having an affair with Von Hohenfels, a dangerous liaison, considering that Eckhart was a married man. This was the leverage Clarkson needed. Müller reported his findings, and just like that, the plan began to take shape."

He took a measured sip of his drink before continuing.

"Müller then approached Von Hohenfels with what seemed like an innocuous, even flattering, proposal, an offer of 150,000 Swiss francs in exchange for allowing him to take some discreet photographs of her with her lover, Eckhart. Naturally, Eckhart would remain completely unaware of this arrangement. Müller assured her that the images were purely for a private collector with a taste for such 'art' and that they would never be seen by anyone else."

"Of course, that was a lie. Clarkson had no art collector, nor any intention of keeping those photographs private. What he had, however, was the perfect setup for blackmail, and the final piece of his plan was about to fall neatly into place."

Adrian concluded his presentation with a slight shrug, his fingers drumming thoughtfully on the table.

"Of course," he admitted, "this is all educated conjecture. I cannot say with absolute certainty how Eckhart might have manipulated the snow depth readings at critical locations, but given his position and access, I have no doubt that it was possible. The system relies heavily on human input, and with the right knowledge and motivation, especially under duress, tampering with the data wouldn't be difficult."

He paused, glancing at the faces around the table before continuing.

"As for the actual execution of the avalanche... well, I can only assume that Eckhart was responsible for that as well. Whether he manually triggered detonations, altered existing controlled explosion plans, or even timed it to coincide with natural instability, the result was the same, devastation, loss of life, and the convenient clearing of a path for Prince Arnold's ascension."

Adrian sighed, swirling the remaining liquid in his glass before taking a final sip.

"But the truth, the absolute truth, may have died with Müller and Clarkson. Unless Eckhart himself provides the missing pieces, we may never know the full extent of their plan."

He placed his glass down with a quiet clink and leaned back in his chair.

"And that, gentlemen, is my theory." Concluded Adrian.

The following morning's meeting was held in the private chambers of the palace, attended by the King, the Queen, and HRH Prince Arnold. Mathew sat in silence as His Majesty addressed him, his tone formal yet filled with gratitude.

"Mathew," the King began, his piercing gaze fixed on him, "we find ourselves at the conclusion of an extraordinary and troubling chapter. I wish to personally thank you for your brilliant investigative work. You have not only helped unravel the mystery of the avalanche but have also exposed the true nature of Melvin Clarkson, assisted the police in apprehending Blair Washington's murderer, and uncovered a long-standing breach within the royal household."

The King exhaled deeply, glancing briefly at his wife, who sat beside him with an expression of quiet dignity.

"Prince Arnold has now been welcomed back into the fold," he continued, gesturing toward the young man seated to his right. "Under the guidance and love of his mother, he will begin the process of rebuilding his standing and his future."

Mathew glanced at the prince, noting the change in his demeanour. Gone was the defiance, the restless arrogance. In its place was something quieter, perhaps even contrite.

"However," the King said, his voice turning heavier, "not all matters have concluded as I had wished. Parliament has formally declined my petition to annul my abdication. Their decision stands, my reign is over. Furthermore," he hesitated for only a moment before pressing on, "they have also refused to recognise you, Prince Mathew, as the legitimate heir to the throne."

Silence hung in the room. Mathew absorbed the words without reaction. He had suspected as much. The weight of history, tradition, and political manoeuvring was too great to be overturned by recent revelations alone.

The Queen reached for her son's hand, giving it a reassuring squeeze. Prince Arnold, though clearly affected by the decision, gave a small nod of understanding.

The King straightened in his chair, his regal bearing undiminished. "Nevertheless, what you have accomplished will not be forgotten. You have served the Crown with honour, and for that, you have our deepest gratitude."

Mathew inclined his head in acknowledgment. The game of power had played out, the cards had been dealt, and now, all that remained was the final reckoning.

Your presence with the royal household is no longer required.

A Moonlit Night

The thick clouds that had shrouded the moon had finally drifted away, revealing its full brilliance. The silver light poured over the camp, illuminating the landscape so intensely that the cicadas, fooled into thinking dawn had arrived, began their high-pitched drone. The once-roaring campfire had dwindled to a bed of glowing embers, pulsating with warmth and hunger for more firewood. Yet, not a single one of the twenty-five people gathered around it, gave it a second glance.

All eyes were locked on the storyteller.

"Well, I couldn't see any future in hanging around there, so here I am!…back in Australia, and that, ladies and gentlemen," Matty declared, leaning back with a satisfied grin, "is how I spent my last Christmas holidays." He paused for dramatic effect, then shook his head. "But, by the jingy, it gets cold in Pommy Land!"

A ripple of laughter rolled through the group, some shaking their heads in amusement while others exchanged knowing glances.

Matty stretched, letting out a yawn before rising to his feet. "Right then, that's enough from me. Goodnight, all! And don't forget, close the flaps of your tents unless you fancy waking up with a snake for a bedmate."

A few gasps, followed by nervous chuckles, filled the air as some of the campers instinctively glanced toward their tents. Matty simply smirked, tipped an imaginary hat, and strolled off into the moonlit night.

End….

Did you enjoy this book?...

If so please tell your friends and I would appreciate it greatly if you could rate it.

Thanks! ... Max

Max Barrington

Other Books By Max Barrington

Woolgar River Park

Task

Dying To Find Gold

Harry Croft

The New March

Bad Company

The First Ten Years in Australia

Fifty Five More Years

You Couldn't Make This Stuff Up

The Writer & The Written

What's Mine is Yours

The Darkie's Gold

The Intrusion

The Premonition

Revelation at Narern

The Telephone

Going Backwards

  Max Barrington

www.ingramcontent.com/pod-product-compliance
Lightning Source LLC
Chambersburg PA
CBHW060602190726
48283CB00003B/1119